EXPOSED

CHIQUITA DENNIE

Visit the official website at www.chiquitadennie.com

Editor: Darlene Tallman

Proofreader: Virginia Tesi Carey

This book is dedicated to my family, especially Rhonda Dennie, Grandma, and Aunt Marcia for always believing in me. Also, I want to shout out my big brother Brent Dennie, JD, Christopher, Lil James, Jazzypoo, my sisters, and best friends from Memphis. Also, to all my LA besties for always supporting me. Shout out to all of my nieces and nephews.

LETTER TO THE READER

Letter to the reader: I wrote Exposed because I love the world of finding two people that seem to always have to fight to be together either by the individual person or the outside world. That's what the Salvation Society means to me, overcoming the fear to fight for what you love. I've included fan favorites Danielle and Mark in my version of a Salvation Society novel. I hope you enjoy a romantic suspense, with a few laughs, a little angst, some sexy times, and a slow burn romance.

DISCLAIMER

This work of fiction contains strong language and explicit sexual content and is only intended for mature readers. This story may contain unconventional situations, language, and sexual encounters that may offend some readers. If you're looking for a sweet, fluffy romance, I would recommend another book. This book is for mature readers (18+).

AUTHOR INSPIRATION

"Never allow anyone to steal your joy. It doesn't matter how many times someone says you can't do something. Invest in yourself—even if it's just writing down what your goals and plans are. Starting small can lead to bigger things."

—Chiquita Dennie

CHARACTER INTERVIEW: LAUREN ARMSTRONG

Today, ladies and gentlemen, we have the fabulous social media influencer, Lauren Armstrong, here with us to discuss her journey in the latest release from author Chiquita Dennie. Welcome to our new installment of character interviews. We look forward to many more, and we love hearing your questions.

Interviewer: So happy you've joined us today. I know you're busy so I'll get right into the questions so readers can start reading about your journey. How do you feel about your story being told?

Lauren: I'm so appreciative of all the work that it took to get the good and bad to be seen. My life was a hell of a ride to write and I'm happy with the finished product.

Interviewer: What would you say is the good and bad?

Lauren: I won't give anything away, but I would say the good is me learning and growing as a person. The bad is what you'll read about for me to get to this space of peace.

Interviewer: So, are you saying that this will leave readers guessing?

Lauren: I'm saying that you should prepare yourselves because the road to a HEA is bumpy.

Interviewer: I hear you became famous by using a hashtag. Is that true?

Lauren: Yep.

Interviewer: Was it love at first sight?

Lauren: Not at all.

Interviewer: For the readers that want to know if you've found Mr. Right in this story and whether his initials start with D.C., can you give us a hint?

Lauren: You never know, Mr. Right could be popping up in this book or another one. You'll just have to read and see.

Interviewer: Can you give us more details?

Lauren: The story is a romantic suspense with a little action, laughs, and a slow burn.

Interviewer: Can you give us one spoiler?

Lauren: Nope.

Interviewer: Tell us who is your favorite makeup line, besides yourself?

Lauren: Easy. Raven Cosmetics.

Interviewer: I know I speak for all the readers when I say that we appreciate you hanging with us today. Readers, enjoy and let us know how Lauren fares in this new release.

CHAPTER ONE

Lauren

"Lauren! Lauren! Can I have an autograph? I'm a huge fan of yours." A fifteen-year-old girl ran up to me, screaming my name. *This was happening to me,* I whispered to myself.

"Yes, of course," I replied. She passed the photo of me posing for *Essence* magazine last month. They held the Annual Breakout Social Media Influencers campaign with four different versions of the most famous stars under thirty. At twenty-five years old, I was living my dream and doing what I loved. It all started off with my YouTube videos and Instagram posts when I trended because of my review of Raven Cosmetics' new natural red lipstick. For an entire week, the hashtag #laurenlovesravencosmetics was the number one trending topic. Now here I am about to go into a meeting with the CEO, Danielle Masters.

"Thank you so much!" she screamed and ran toward her group of friends.

I loved meeting my fans and getting comments, letters, and messages. I know some people like my parents didn't believe this was a real career choice. In their eyes, it wasn't something that could last forever. My goal was to turn this into my business and create my own brand and products one day. I checked one last time that my makeup was still intact and puffed out my hair. As I pulled out Raven Cosmetics' clear lip gloss, my phone rang. I checked and noticed my cousin, Mya, was calling. She was the Governor's wife in New York and probably one day the First Lady if Ethan ran for office again. I hit the FaceTime call, and her flawless, brown skin radiated through the phone.

"Ohh, I like that color on you," Mya said.

I puckered up and blew a kiss through the phone.

"Thanks, cousin. What are you up to?" I asked, opening the door and walking through the lobby.

"I wanted to send you positive thoughts for your meeting."

"Thanks, I wish I knew what this was about. All the email said was that I was meeting with the CEO. My nerves are bad."

"Don't think anything bad; you had the highest trending topic last week. I doubt the meeting could turn bad," Mya replied.

"I needed to hear that. I made it inside. I need to

get my badge and head up; I'll call you afterward," I said, and she blew a kiss back and hung up. I put my phone back in my purse and walked over to the receptionist's desk.

"Hello, welcome to Raven Cosmetics, do you have an appointment?" the brunette receptionist questioned. Glancing around, I noticed the place was very sleek and modern.

"Hi, yes, I have an appointment with Danielle Masters. I'm Lauren Armstrong," I replied.

"Yes, we've been expecting you today. Here's your visitor badge, and you can take the elevator at the end of the hall and go to floor fifteen, and the receptionist will assist you."

"Thank you," I said, grabbing the bright plastic badge with my name across the center. I was happy that I wore my off-shoulder light pink blouse jumpsuit. The large belt and red high heel shoes showed off my style of being modern and feminine, yet professional. Getting on the elevator, I hit the button for the fifteenth floor, and the doors closed. I checked my phone in my clutch to make sure it was on vibrate. Hearing the ding, I looked up to see that I'd arrived. I took one last breath and smiled as the doors opened to a large reception area with Raven Cosmetics signs in the background. Stepping in front of the receptionist's desk, she held a hand up, telling me to wait a second while she ended a call. I looked around the room to notice the large photo of Raven Cosmetics' signature natural line displayed on the wall. A large plasma TV was airing the latest commercial, the sound on low.

"Hi, Lauren Armstrong, right?" the receptionist asked. I looked down at her name tag and read Kasey.

"Yes, I have an appointment with Danielle Masters."

"I know, everyone has been waiting for your arrival."

"Really?"

"Yes. I saw your last video on YouTube where you did the review and paired it with any outfit. I'm a huge fan if you haven't noticed," Kasey said.

"Thanks." I smiled, taking in her compliment.

"Let me buzz Ms. Masters' office."

She picked up the phone and dialed a number I assumed was to Danielle's assistant. A few minutes later, the door opened, and the person I thought was her secretary coming to meet me was actually Danielle Masters. The genuine smile on her face made me automatically feel comfortable as she extended her hand for me to shake.

"Lauren, I'm so excited you came," Danielle said.

"Thank you, I'm still not sure what to expect out of this meeting today. The email said all the details would be discussed when I arrived."

We headed to the clear office door of the employee

area, then down a hall where a row of clear doored offices lined up.

"Sorry, we had to be vague. I wanted to make sure nothing was leaked in the press. Recently our online store was hacked, and we've been going through an overhaul," she responded, escorting me to a conference room. As we walked inside, I saw a group of people that apparently worked for her based on the company badges they wore; there was a woman with short dark brown hair, two others wore lab coats, and another guy who was in a business suit. The two I knew from the company website were the new owner, Elijah Cohen, and the publicist, Zoe Anderson. She used to work at CCJ and came on board full-time to work at Raven Cosmetics. I was confident when I first came down here, and now, I was nervous at what was taking place. Usually, you wouldn't receive any backlash for reviewing a product, so I hoped I wouldn't get sued or something. Danielle introduced me to everyone, and I waved, as the butterflies in my stomach flipped.

"Lauren, again, thank you for coming. I know you're wondering why we asked you to come to Virginia on such short notice," Zoe said.

"Just a little."

Everybody laughed at my statement.

"Well, let me put your mind at ease, you're not in trouble. In fact, we want to hire you. Zoe was very impressed with your work," Danielle spoke, passing over a document with the contract on top.

"Seriously?" I mumbled, hand across my mouth in shock.

"I watched your video and posts, and you have a loyal fan base. Built a nice following with five million followers across your social media platforms. Especially for someone at twenty-five, very impressive."

"I told Danielle about you getting Raven Cosmetics as a trending topic. As PR for the company, we scout out constantly how the brand is doing online and the statistics showed that your review skyrocketed sales up 110% in a day," Zoe advised.

"We would like for you to be a brand ambassador. We're taking Raven Cosmetics to an everyday-women level that loves makeup and style.

"It was Zoe's idea to have Raven on the map as the place to be for all women. Make a more hands-on approach with getting the product to everyday customers, showcasing style and perspective," Danielle said.

"I don't know what to say," I replied.

"Say yes, so this grumpy guy can head back home to his wife and kids," Zoe teased, pointing at Elijah. The entire room laughed as Elijah shrugged his shoulders at her comment.

"I'd love to, and I have so many ideas. Wow, this is incredible," I answered.

"Great! Look over your contract, and how soon can you move down here? I know Virginia is south of New York is your home base, but most of what you'll be doing is here in Virginia. I understand your family is in New York, but the company base is here, so we'd need you to move to Virginia," Danielle stated.

"Not long, maybe a week."

"We can put you up at a hotel until we get you a place to stay. I know you're at

Ocean View Hotel, is that okay for you for the time being? Of course, all of this is on the company," Danielle stated.

"Yes, that works fine."

"That means I can head out and leave you ladies to discuss all the gossip. Welcome to the team, Lauren," Elijah said, before standing up, then leaning over the table to shake my hand.

"Don't listen to him, I'm excited to have you on board. I don't work out of the Virginia office full-time. I have my main publicity business in here for other brands, but I'll pop in every blue moon. Now Danielle is running the company since Elijah bought it from Jackson," Zoe insisted.

"Thank you again." I grinned, trying to keep the excitement from bubbling up and freaking everyone out.

"We will see you in a week, Lauren, please don't hesitate to call me if you need anything right away.

Here's my personal number in case of an emergency. Kasey will give you all of your details on your way out," Danielle told me. I shook her hand again and grabbed the paperwork leaving the conference room. I headed to Kasey's desk.

"All set?" Kasey questioned.

"I am. Danielle told me you'd have some information for me."

"Oh yes, here's your flight information and hotel. We will have you in the same room suite when you return. They will give you a driver and company card when you sign off on your contract."

"I'm really working at Raven Cosmetics," I stated.

"I can't wait to see what you come up with."

"Me too."

I walked toward the elevator, stepped on and hit the button to go back down. I pulled my phone out of my purse and dialed my cousin's number, keeping my head low. A few minutes later, it came to my destination and I stepped off and ran into a hard body.

"Ouch!" I shouted. I pressed my hand on top of his arms to prevent him from falling down and instead, I ended up dropping my phone.

"Are you okay?" I heard a deep, smooth, seductive voice question.

"Have you ever heard of elevator etiquette?" I questioned, peering up into the most enchanting brown eyes glaring back at me.

"Have you ever heard of paying attention to where you're going? Maybe if you stayed off your phone, you'd notice other people," he spat, moving around me into the elevator. I wanted to curse him out, but I was on a serious show and didn't need that type of negativity in my space at the moment. I pulled my shades out of my purse and walked out of the building to my awaiting car. I jumped inside and headed back to the hotel to catch a flight home to pack.

CHAPTER TWO

Lauren

One week later, I was packing my things to prepare to head back to Virginia for my new life. The announcement about me becoming the new face of Raven Cosmetics was all over social media. I would not only promote in magazines, online, and host events, I would have the opportunity to be hands-on with the creation of products for my own line down the road.

Hearing a knock on my door, I yelled to come inside as I zipped up my last bag before I placed it at the front door. My mother opened the door and walked inside, holding containers of food.

"Do you need any help?" she asked, walking into the kitchen, putting the food in the fridge. She removed her jacket and purse, sitting down on the couch in the living room. Peering around the room, I sighed in exhaustion before pouring myself a glass of wine.

"No, I have everything, the hotel has my room set, and I'll move into my apartment in a few days." I grabbed my phone, turning it on silent as notifications continued going off.

"I know we've been tough on you about your life choices. Your father and I love you, Lauren, we wish you'd think twice about moving to another state on your own." At five-seven, with golden brown skin, full lips, and a button nose, I really took after my father; people called me his twin. Kenny Armstrong, a proud construction worker, and my mom, Vivien Armstrong, stayed at home to raise us. All my life, they'd instilled that school was important, and I should focus on being a doctor or lawyer, something that's reliable and real. Growing up in a household where you didn't have much and getting bullied at school, my confidence dwindled when the boys only used me for one thing and learning that I didn't need to try to impress people to get them to love me took a few years for me to grow out of that headspace. I made a lot of my clothes, wanting to be stylish even though we weren't rich. I wanted to do something that would bring me happiness, and it wasn't my fault that I fell in love with makeup while watching my mother get ready whenever my father took her out on a date. I have one younger brother that's seventeen, Kenny Jr., the class clown that always ends up in some type of trouble. He's excited about this opportunity and wants to move with me, but I told him maybe in a year after I get settled and he graduates school. The last thing I need is to babysit a kid that's at the age of not wanting to listen to anyone.

The small resemblances that I take from my mom would have to be my attitude and maybe never admitting when you are wrong. She told me years ago how she went to school to be a writer and gave up on her dream because she needed to help feed her family, and then, she fell in love with my dad and got pregnant, so all of her dreams went away and she became a wife, a mother, and a nurse. I know she loves her job, but if she was ever given a chance, I wonder if she would take it.

"Do you ever think about writing again?"

She waved me off and stood, putting her hands on her hips, then pointing in my face.

"Grow up, Lauren, there is no future in this fairy tale lifestyle you're doing. How many times do I have to say it to you? Baby, I don't want you to be disappointed." She lifted my chin, caressing my cheek. I closed my eyes and pulled back, and stood up, hugging her.

"I love you, Ma, but I need to do this. I'm not you, and I won't let love distract me from my goals. Mya was able to get her career off the ground, and now she's a famous TV show host and wife to the Governor."

"She was lucky, I guess, but Mya's not my child. You are, and I hate that you're moving away. If you're going to do this, at least keep me updated with everything, and then, I will be out to visit you once you're settled."

"Thank you, and I'll call you tomorrow after I get in and rest up." My mother nodded, kissed me on the cheek, then headed toward the door. She looked back at me, and I blew a kiss toward her as the door shut. This was my new beginning. I could only go up from here. I picked up my phone and saw a text message from an unknown number.

Unknown: Congrats!

Me: Who is this?

Unknown: Lauren, you're the best!

I figured it was a friend playing on my phone, so I replied back, thanks, and continued cleaning up my living room for the rest of the night.

Monday morning, I was putting on my makeup in front of the mirror in my hotel suite. Today was my first day of doing a tour of the facility and meeting the Raven Cosmetics team. Danielle emailed a schedule of everything I'd be doing for the rest of the week from blog interviews, radio station visits, and photoshoots, and I was hoping to have a little time to find a permanent place to stay in Virginia. My best friend was planning on moving down here with me next month, and I couldn't wait to have a familiar person around here. Novah was the complete opposite of me, but we've been friends since middle school. Novah Gibbs studied to be an accountant and recently transferred out here to start her own business. Like me, she was single at twenty-five and not looking to fall for the first guy she came across. I snapped a new photo with my favorite pink gloss and posted it on my page. I brushed my hair into a high bun, grabbed my black leather jacket off my bed, and strolled toward the door. Raven Cosmetics had a car waiting for me outside, so I didn't need to worry about a ride. Ten minutes later, I stepped out of the hotel and waved to my driver, Carl.

"Hi, Carl."

"Miss Armstrong."

He held the door open, and I slid inside. Carl's an older gentleman, he reminded me of my grandfather. He was always dropping some type of knowledge and wisdom about life. Driving off into traffic, I send a text to Novah to let her know all of the arrangements were set for her to arrive.

"Are you excited for today, Miss Armstrong?" Carl questioned, signaling to let a driver get ahead of him in the left lane.

"I am, my fans are ready to see what I come up with and I have all my notes in my phone of different ideas for colors and schemes for the layout. This is the first time this has happened where a non-celebrity, non-model has ever won an endorsement deal for a makeup company off of a trending hashtag. Usually, they send you some gifts or something, but I actually got hired as a spokesperson to give my opinion," I told him.

"My granddaughter is a huge fan of yours."

"Really? Tell her I said hello."

Carl nodded and pulled up to the gate of the building and showed his ID. The guard let him inside, and we pulled up to the parking structure of the building. I looked around at the outside construction of the building, and it seemed more like a campus than an office building. The door opened a few seconds later, and I stepped out thanking Carl again. Danielle was standing at the receptionist's desk, and I walked over, extending a hand out.

"Hi, Lauren, you look amazing, as usual," Danielle stated.

"You look beautiful as well. This place is gorgeous.

I can already see some ideas forming in my brain to post," I replied, following behind her.

"Thanks, follow me back here so I can give you a tour. We have a conference call with Zoe and Elijah after lunch, and then you have a photoshoot," Danielle said, opening the door to an office.

"This will be your office space when you come in for shoots or interviews. I told them to decorate it based on your style from your social pages. Hopefully, it's okay."

The place was gorgeous with a modern, classic feel, open spaces, and ergonomic furniture. It was done in cream and pink colors, had a glass desk, a couch, and a small fridge in the corner. Paintings on the wall of Raven Cosmetics products were a nice touch and complemented the room beautifully.

"I love the style, and I look forward to really making my mark with this opportunity, Danielle."

"I believe you. We can go to the lab and see what they're cooking up."

"That will be perfect. Is it possible for me to get a few shots of me in the lab? Of course, I'll cover up any major details. I think giving my fans an inside look and what I do will draw interest."

"I trust you," Danielle answered.

As we continued walking down the hall, I saw the same guy I ran into talking with Elijah in his office. It looked pretty intense, and I wanted to be nosy and ask what he was doing here, but I remembered he was coming inside the building that day, so he might have worked here or something.

Danielle swiped her badge to open the door and said, "This is our lab where we test our products. You will find yourself meeting with them more than anyone else in the building besides myself. I want you to get familiar." Two girls and a guy in lab coats came over and shook my hand.

"Hi, I'm Carol, the team leader, this is Ben and Josslyn," Carol said, motioning between the three of them.

"Nice to meet you guys."

"Okay so the first order of business is getting you familiar with our new spring collection. Ready to work?" Danielle asked, and I gave a thumbs up when Ben passed me a pair of clear goggles and a lab coat.

CHAPTER THREE

Dominic

"Why am I just now hearing about this? Does Jackson know?" I questioned, turning the next document over. Mark called me a few weeks back about doing some private security for the company after it was sold to Elijah. We had a conference call with Danielle when she brought up her concerns to Mark. As a CEO of the company, Danielle requested I step in and assist with everything that's happening at the moment. Much to my surprise, the girl I ran into on the elevator was the new ambassador for the company. It made sense why she was so obnoxious when we first met. She had her nose stuck up in the air. I worked as a freelance private contractor for Cole Security. My business partner Emmanuel and I are looking into eventually starting our own Security and Intelligence Agency firm full-time, since we left the Navy years ago. That's how I knew Mark and Jackson. I was there the day he got shot, seeing his body fall to the ground is a day I never want to witness again. Going to war and watching your brothers get picked off one by one was no easy thing to see. We all have marks on our bodies, reminding us of the fallen. Emmanuel was single like me and running from his demons of our past time from war. He was better at managing his emotions than me at times or at least he pretended to be. At thirty-four years old, he's like a little brother to me and I'd give my life for his, hell, for Mark or Jackson as well.

"Shooter, you know I wanted to get in touch with you sooner. Danielle thought it was a mistake on their end and didn't think anything was really wrong," Mark said, calling me by my SEAL name that I earned because every time I drew my weapon, I hit the enemy right between the eyes the first time. All of us had a nickname – Mark was called Twilight, Jackson got the name Muffin, shortened to Muff, Emmanuel was Stinger. That day Jackson got the call to go back to get Aaron's body was the day everyone met back up and the old crew was back in sync. Meeting Catherine and Danielle through Mark and Jackson was a blessing, I felt like they were not only my friends, but little sisters to me. Jackson had told us about Neil acting like a bitch that one time and making it seem like they were still together. He told us about the confrontation and kicking his ass in front of her apartment.

Now at thirty-six, I was focused on building a life for myself without any drama. Women were the least of my worries right now. I did have people that I could call if I need to relieve some stress, but my overall agenda wasn't to fall in love. Oftentimes they did, and then I had to move on. Jacinda made the mistake of betraying my trust and caused me to look at every woman the same. They will only want you for what you can give them, and I refused to fall in love with another one.

"Let me think about it, Twilight, this could be a big job, and I need more time to screen everyone in the company all the way to the mail carriers that the company uses," I stated, treading to the bar and pouring a glass of whiskey.

"Pretty early for that, don't you think?" Mark asked. I shrugged, not caring what he thought. Mark was always checking in on us as the big brother of the group. He got on my nerves most times. I appreciated him for keeping me in check, but when I need a drink, I'm having a drink.

"Don't start."

"That's my job."

"Jackson says the same thing," I said, pouring another shot.

"Jackson is fine, I'm fine. Stop worrying about things you can't control. We all look back on those days and second-guess ourselves. Listen, Charlie wants to set you up on a date. Maybe getting a woman will help you calm down." Mark chuckled. His wife was always trying to find me a woman. She thinks I'm wasting my time with all the women I juggle. I flipped him off, and out of the corner of my eye, I saw the same girl that I ran into walking in behind Danielle.

"Glad you are still here, Dominic," Danielle said. I could tell right off the bat this was going to be a conversation I didn't want to have. She stood a few inches shorter than my six-one height, but still tall enough that I could bend her over and spank her ass if she got out of line. What the hell am I saying? She glared at me, and I chuckled, putting the shot glass down and sliding my hands into my pockets. The tension was high in the room, and I didn't want to start off the day pissing off one of my best friend's clients.

"Dominic Combs, meet our new ambassador, Lauren Armstrong. You two will be working closely together over the next few months to a year," Danielle stated. I guess she was thinking like me and didn't want to be in the same room as she started shaking her head no.

"Danielle, I don't need a bodyguard. I can take care

of myself." Lauren started folding her arms across her chest. Narrowing her eyes, she was generally resentful of the situation. My brow drew downward in a frown.

"You heard the princess. She doesn't need my help," I remarked, picking up the file folder off Elijah's desk, preparing to leave the office when Danielle stopped me.

"Wait for Dominic, when you leave Lauren, you will need some form of protection. I know you feel like your fans are a family, but going into the amount of publicity we plan for this launch, you need security, and Dominic is the best. I trust him, and Jackson wouldn't have sent him if he didn't think he could protect you on the road," Danielle replied. I sighed in annoyance. I had plans to meet up with my brother for a game of basketball, and I was running late.

"Read over the rest of the file, Shooter, and let us know if you need anything. She officially starts whatever it is she does this week," Mark announced.

"Wait, you've already scheduled her for travel? Why wasn't I told about this?" I demanded, furrowing my brow.

"I asked Danielle to start asap. I told her to call Mark for help," Elijah told me.

I watched as the Lauren chick shoved her hands in the air, pissed off.

"Hello, *she* is right here, and I don't need to get

permission from anyone before going somewhere. Kenny and Vivien Armstrong live in New York."

"Now you're under my watch, so that changes today," I told her, stalking over, closing the space between us. She didn't back down, and I sure as hell wasn't going to let some pampered princess tell me how to do my job. She pointed her manicured nail in my face. "This isn't the Army. I suggest you take that up with someone who cares," she spat back, her gaze boring into my eyes.

"I feel like there's more to you two than him being your bodyguard. Are we missing something?" Danielle questioned.

"Yeah, I'd like to know that as well. It was the Navy, Lauren, and he's my old SEAL team member," Mark instigated, folding his arms.

"He has no elevator etiquette," Lauren commented.

"And you have no awareness of your surroundings. If you paid more attention to your surroundings and less on what was happening on your phone, you'd know the door had opened," I growled, crossing my arms.

"Wait, you bumped into each other on the elevator, and you're pissed about it?"

"He didn't say sorry, excuse me, my bad, zilch," Lauren remarked.

Danielle and Mark busted out in laughter, and I observed the amusement on their faces.

"That's not funny," I said, running a hand down my face.

"I agree with him on that. Danielle, you're supposed to be on my side," Lauren said, which caused Mark and Danielle to laugh even louder.

"Shooter, you have to take this job. I can already see the fireworks kicking off. Wait till I tell Jackson and Catherine," Mark replied, patting me on the back, swaggering out of the office.

"I'm sorry, Lauren, but this was too funny. I promise Dominic won't get in your way. He's only here to protect you. Right, Dominic?" Danielle questioned.

"If I decide to take the case, I will do my best to not get in your way, Mrs. Armstrong."

"Miss Armstrong. I'm not married," she replied and walked out of the room. Danielle shook her head and giggled, as I watched the most aggravating woman I'd ever met, piss me off in less than five minutes.

"Well, I see you two will get along great," Danielle teased.

"Call someone else," I announced, dropping the file folder back down on the desk.

"Dominic, we wouldn't ask you if it wasn't that important," Elijah said.

"Dominic! Come on. Lauren's nice. Yes, she's young, but I think she's great for the company. We need the best, and you're the best person to keep things running smoothly. Please!"

"How old is she?" I asked.

"Twenty-five," she mumbled under her breath.

"I figured between twenty-two and twenty-six. I'm no babysitter, Danielle, you know me, and I don't take crap from anyone. When I say it's time to go, we leave and I suggest you let her know. I'm not on her payroll," I stated and walked out, not waiting for an answer.

CHAPTER FOUR

Dominic

As soon as I left, I called my brother to let him know that I was running late for the basketball game he set up with our friends. It was normally three on three, and Mark usually joined us, but he had some work to do at Cole Security. I pulled into the parking space at the park and grabbed my gym bag out of the back seat and jogged up to the basketball court right as they were going into a time out. Desmond Combs is my older brother at thirty-eight; he works as a police officer for the Virginia Police Department. Our father is a retired Army man and police officer, so we both took after him in wanting to help people. My mother was a stay-at-home mother raising two boys and a girl. Little sister's in college for her bachelor's in music, and at first, my parents weren't happy about her wanting to be a singer, but in time they came around and got on board. Lauren reminded me of my sister, Devan. Partially my and Desmond's fault because we gave her anything she wanted and never said no. We could never turn down those big brown eyes when she was a kid, and now at twenty-one, I prayed for the man that ended up marrying her because he'd have a lot to live up to.

"I see you finally showed up," Desmond said, fist-bumping me as I removed my bag and grabbed the ball out of his hands.

"Yeah, I had a meeting that ran over at Raven Cosmetics."

"What about?" Desmond questioned, guzzling down the water.

"They need me to bodyguard a client of theirs."

Elias, our cousin and jokester of the group, just got slapped by a group of women, and I shook my head as he walked over, rubbing his face.

"That's your problem, always trying to get laid," I commented.

"Man, she wasn't cute anyway. What's up with you? You're late," Elias retorted.

"I just asked that, idiot," Desmond responded, and popped him in the back of the head.

"Motherfucker!" Elias yelled, play slapping him back. Elias was only around five-seven to my brother and my heights of six-one and six-three. His lack of height was replaced with jokes, and he became the class clown in our group while growing up. Both of us were single, and Desmond was married with three kids of his own. Two boys and a girl. I heard it almost every day from my mom about having more grandchildren, and I politely ignored her because I refused to have any children without being married just to please her, and the women I've noticed lately only wanted a man for the money and status.

"Yeah, my bad. I was telling Desmond I just left a meeting with Mark about bodyguarding a new client."

"Is she hot?" Elias asked, wiggling his eyebrows.

"That's the only thing you worry about?" I answered.

"I mean, you have to be around her all day. Shit, at least let her be sexy. Wait, unless it's a guy?" Elias queried, hands on his hips. Shaking my head no, I replied, "A woman and I'm debating taking the case. She's some social media celebrity that does nothing all day but take photos." I spat my words out, still aggravated over the meeting itself as well as her attitude, bouncing the ball between my legs. Elias snapped his fingers. "Wait, she's famous for taking pictures all day, and she got hired by a makeup company. Ohhhh... Shit! It's Lauren Armstrong, right?" Elias asked, excitedly.

Desmond and I gawked at his animated reaction.

"Uhm, yeah. I take it you follow her."

He pulled his phone out of his pocket and scrolled, looking for something. A second later, he showed us a picture of Lauren wearing lingerie posing in the mirror. She had her ass and titties out for the world to see; her golden-brown skin glowed against the red one piece. I grabbed the phone out of his hand, pissed that he saw her so intimately. I would never let my woman do shit like this and think it was for everybody to see.

"Delete the photo," I told him.

He chuckled, shaking his head. "Man, I'm not deleting this, besides it came from her social media account. Everybody can see it. What's the big deal?"

"Bro, you got a crush on little Miss Lauren?" Desmond wondered.

"Are we playing ball or not?" I glared at them both.

Desmond and Elias cracked up, laughing at my expense.

"Fuck y'all!" I said, walking toward the court, and Desmond pulled me back, wrapping his arm around my shoulder.

"All right, all right, my bad. She looks good, young though. Stop tripping, if you like her, that's cool. I know Jacinda did a number on you four years ago, but you need to move on," Desmond stated, stealing the ball out of my hands as we walked to the court.

"Desmond's right, D. Jacinda ain't worth cutting all that your future wife can make up for. If you don't like Lauren, at least put in a good word for me," Elias joked. I tried to get out of my brother's hold to kick Elias's ass, and he ran off the court.

"Fuck you, Elias! I don't like that girl. Unlike you, a big butt and a smile don't impress me," I said, picking up the ball and shooting it in the hoop. Desmond passed the ball back to me, and I dribbled down the court and dunked it inside.

"That's all I need in life. A big butt, a nice small waist, and a good home-cooked meal, and I am satisfied," Elias yelled twenty feet away.

"Auntie must have dropped you on your head when you were born."

"Y'all just jealous all the ladies love my sexiness," Elias insisted, removing his shirt, trying to show off his muscles that clearly never came in because all I saw was a beer belly.

"On that note, we need to finish this game so we can get dinner at our parents' house," Desmond informed us.

I checked my watch, and saw it was going on six o'clock.

"When did I agree to dinner?"

"When your mother became Sonya Combs," Desmond teased, stealing the ball away from me.

"Auntie Sonya don't play. Either you're on life support or heading to the ER, otherwise you better be at her dinner table when she requests you." Elias laughed, and I nodded, knowing he was right. Growing up, she was the drill sergeant and made sure we had food on the table and clothes on our backs. I loved my mother, giving her anything she wanted. But the woman could be overbearing at times, probably why my dad gave in 99% of the time to avoid pissing her off. She had a habit of ignoring him, and the moment that happened, my dad would be pissed because he hated being ignored. That was something we had in common and I tried my best not to let it get to me.

"What time is dinner at?" I inquired.

"In an hour. I have to go get the kids from the center and pick up Joyce," Desmond answered, looking at his watch.

"Cool, let's finish this round really quickly and then leave," I said.

Taking out the trash at my parents' house as my mother argued about me being late to dinner was not how I wanted to spend my evening. Devan was setting the table with my niece, Joi, as my two nephews, Chris and JD, played the PS4 game that I bought them a few months back. They had rooms here at my parents' house, as well as at my place when they spent the night —all the exact same things to keep the fighting down. I remembered Desmond and I fighting when we were little over Pac-Man games and his bike. We've come full circle, and looking into their eyes, I felt proud of how they were growing up.

"Dominic, are you listening to me?" Sonya asked, wiping her hands on the dish towel. She made her famous pot roast, green beans, salad, turnips, and red velvet cake.

"Of course, I'm listening, beautiful," I responded, kissing her on the forehead.

"Boy, I'm not one of your little playthings, you can't smile at me and expect I'll fall in line. I'm your mother, I know when you're lying to get me off your back," she chastised.

I chuckled, wrapping my arm around her shoulder, kissing her cheek.

"I see the reason why dinner isn't ready yet. You're up here talking to this knucklehead," my dad commented. Drake Combs, my father, was taller than my brother and me. At six-five, he was a big man that commanded the room when he walked inside. Everyone could tell you a story about Drake 'Smooth' Combs. He received that nickname when he was in the Army because he was smooth with disarming the enemy. You'd never see it coming. He just had a steady personality that made you want to confess your problems so he could solve them for you.

"Old man, your woman won't leave me alone," I fussed, winking at her to play along.

"Old Man! Boy, I'll show you old. I can take you right now. School you on a few things," he joked, pretending to fight box. My mother waved him off and pushed me away.

"Drake, go sit down somewhere, dinner is coming out. I swear all you think about is food," Sonya fussed. He laughed and reached out to wrap her in his arms, he squeezed her closer, nuzzling his face in her neck and she giggled.

"Please, let's not do this in front of your son. You two are too old for that mess," I argued, turning to walk out of the kitchen.

"How does he think he got in this world?" I heard behind my back.

The rest of the evening we laughed, the kids played games, and we caught up with everyone's day. I ended up sleeping at my parents' house that night rather than driving home late.

CHAPTER FIVE

Lauren

One week later, Novah and I were having breakfast in our new condo that I found. She came down earlier than expected and surprised me, so she helped me to pack up and get things moved in, and I felt better now than living out of a suitcase every day. The place wasn't too far from Raven Cosmetics and the hot spots of Virginia. Basically, I had the benefits of both worlds.

"So tell me about this bodyguard again."

"Not much to say. He's officially to start with me today, I guess. In the last few days, he had someone else with me whenever I needed to go shopping at the mall or something. I prefer Emmanuel, his partner. He's less intense than Dominic," I said, soaking a piece of the biscuit in the syrup. Having a best friend that loved to cook was another reason I'm glad she decided to move. I can cook simple things like eggs, bacon, and hamburgers. The cooking habits skipped over me and went to my brother. KJ loves to cook, and I'm trying to convince him to go to culinary school.

"Is he cute, at least?" Novah asked.

"I mean, he's okay looking," I muttered, lying through my teeth, remembering his large broad shoulders in the suit he wore in the office yesterday. It made me think about what was underneath. He looked like he worked out religiously.

"You said that really low, which tells me he must be hot as fuck, and you're pissed that you like him. Am I right?"

"I don't like him. He has no elevator etiquette."

"So?"

"So. That tells me everything I need to know about him, shit he's probably selfish in other ways that I will never know about." I gulped the orange juice.

"That happened almost a month ago, and you're still holding grudges. Lauren, get over yourself."

"Bitch!" I threw my napkin at her.

"It's true but describe your bodyguard boyfriend."

"The typical tall, chestnut brown skin, chiseled cheekbones, straight white teeth, full lips perfect for pussy eating, with a five o'clock shadow, low-cut fade and about six-one or two in height, large calloused hands, but soft at the same time and a big, athletic build broad shoulders. Nothing to write home about."

"Wow! What about his hands?" Novah queried, fanning herself.

"I didn't really get a good look, but they looked big."

"You know they say a guy with big hands and clean nails is a keeper," Novah said, picking up her glass of orange juice.

"You're being overdramatic, Novah, and he looks like any normal guy we come across."

"I doubt that, and even with you not liking him, you sure as hell described him to a tee."

I rolled my eyes at her comment.

"I'm good at noticing people's looks. What can I say? It's a gift and a curse. But that man is the last thing on my mind."

"Sure, Lauren. What else is happening for you?"

"I have a photoshoot today at the beach for Raven Cosmetics, and they're letting me hold a giveaway to allow a few winners to come to the launch party."

"That's great. What time do you have to be at the beach?" Novah asked, checking the time on the stove.

"Around eleven, are you coming?" I asked, switching from Instagram to Snapchat.

"I can come for moral support. I don't start working for another week," Novah responded, standing up, grabbing our plates to clean the dishes.

"Perfect! Like old times, wear something sexy!" I

yelled over my shoulder, running to my bedroom to grab things.

Opening my closet, I grabbed my sandals and t-shirt to cover up my bathing suit. I had it personally made from another social media designer; we've worked together in the past, and I had her add Raven Cosmetics across the top. It perfectly matched the details of the photoshoot I have to attend. Picking up my iPad, I noticed I had a few concepts that Danielle sent over along with the photographer. Checking my phone one last time, I saw another message from an unknown number.

Unknown: Excited for your shoot.

Me: Who is this?

Unknown: Your number one fan.

Thinking about it, I figured it could be an ex-boyfriend I dumped and blocked a few months back who was trying to get back together.

Me: Whatever, Raymond. Leave me alone.

I replied back and blocked them from my phone. Walking into the living room, Novah was standing at the door.

"What are you looking at?" I questioned.

"I was thinking this place is huge for the amount of money we pay compared to New York apartments."

I agreed and followed her out, shutting and locking the door. Heading out toward my car, I passed her the keys so I could stay on top of responding to my fans that commented on my photos.

"Type in the address of the location," Novah asked.

"Ohh, I almost forgot. Have you heard from Raymond? I think he's playing on my phone."

"No, what do you mean playing on your phone?"

"This is the second time I received a text message from an unknown number saying they're my biggest fan and congratulating me on winning the Raven deal."

"That is strange. Probably a good thing your sexy bodyguard can help you out."

"Ha-ha, you're not funny," I said, rolling my eyes. She backed up, pulling out of the parking space, driving off toward the beach.

Forty minutes later, we arrived at the beach. A few trucks were lined up on the beach with the Raven Cosmetics logo as well as the film crew. I noticed Danielle talking to Josslyn; I saw the makeup trailer next to a sign that read Raven 'Private Events Only'.

"Here we are," Novah said, turning the car off. Grabbing our bags from the back, we walked over to Danielle as she gave directions to the caterers.

"This is looking good, Danielle," I said, giving her a hug.

"Thank you. I'm excited Zoe came up with the beach idea. We will probably have the next one inside," Danielle replied.

"Sounds great. I'm ready, maybe a little touch-up."

"Today you're taking photos of lipstick and body glitter. Do you have your swimsuit?" Danielle questioned.

"All set. Actually, I'm wearing it right now." I passed my bag to Novah and removed my shirt and shorts. As soon as I removed the shirt, I heard whispers behind me.

"What the hell are you wearing?!" I jumped at the interruption.

"Dominic, you came. I'm so glad," Danielle stated, clapping her hands together.

"She's not shooting in that." He removed his jacket and tried to cover me up. I rolled my eyes and pushed his jacket away.

"We're on the beach. There's nothing wrong with my swimsuit." I tried to walk off with Novah, and he stepped in front of me.

"You're selling lipstick; you don't need a thong for that," Dominic argued, stopping a crew member and grabbing the robe out of his hands to cover me up.

"Hi, I'm Novah," Novah said, extending her hand to Dominic.

"Dominic Combs," he responded, smiling in her face. I glanced between the two and saw Novah blushing and I felt a hint of jealousy.

"Novah! Let's go." I pushed her forward, trying to get her to leave.

"Hold up. Danielle, she needs to cover up. She's showing off too much skin," Dominic stated.

I was trying to compose myself and not go off on him in front of the others and be seen as the diva.

"I'm wearing my swimsuit, nothing's wrong with me wearing a thong. I'm selling a product, and my fans want to see my outfit. You need to loosen up more, grab a drink and chill," I advised, patting his chest and walking off. I heard giggling behind me and saw Danielle shaking her head at both of us.

CHAPTER SIX

Lauren

I slammed the trailer door and paced back and forth. Novah cackled, sitting down in the chair at the vanity mirror as the hairdresser started removing the hair products out of her bag.

"He's cute," Novah remarked.

"Not funny."

"Lauren, are you keeping your hair up?" Lia asked.

"Yeah, Danielle wants to do a body glow, and I hate to get my hair messed up."

"She's grumpy because her bodyguard boyfriend yelled at her," Novah said, tossing her hair into a ponytail. Lia chuckled, plugging in the curling iron and setting up the makeup station.

"Which one? I saw about four or five guys out there walking around," Lia replied.

"The tall one with the full lips and a low-cut fade.

Can you bump my ends for me?" Novah asked. Lia nodded.

"I understand this is amusing for you, Novah, but get out of my seat."

Lia and Novah laughed at me, and I flipped them both off. The door opened, and Dominic came inside. Novah mumbled 'trouble' under her breath.

"Get out," I demanded.

"Gladly, but first, let's get something straight. When it comes to my job it means you listen to what I have to say and follow my orders. You're not wearing that outfit. I already told Danielle you're changing or wearing a cover-up," Dominic informed me.

"What type of swimsuit are you wearing?" Lia questioned.

"A string," he answered.

"A one piece," I remarked.

I removed my robe and stood in front of his face, with my hands on my hips. I heard giggling behind me. He smirked, getting a rise out of pushing my buttons.

"Listen, Dominic. I suggest you go secure something or someone that needs your services. I'm fine over here and not changing my mind." A knock on the trailer door came, and I yelled, "Come inside." A young assistant, probably no more than twenty, was carrying a tray of food. He smiled at me and tried to move around Dominic, only he refused to move.

"Hey, Lauren, I brought some lunch for you guys," the assistant said.

"Leave it and go," Dominic told him.

"Ummmm," the assistant hesitantly said, looking between the two of us.

"You can stay," I responded, trying to reach around him.

"If you want to keep your job, you'll drop the food and leave now," Dominic spat, turning and glaring at him.

The production assistant dropped the food and ran out, causing Novah and Lia to laugh out loud.

"I like you," Novah said to Dominic.

"Thanks, if only your friend would listen to me, then I could do my job properly," Dominic stated, crossing his arms while peering into my eyes and licking his lips.

"You-" I was stuck staring back into his eyes. I was torn on why I couldn't stop watching the way he gazed at me. A flutter in my stomach was something I wasn't familiar with. I wanted to continue challenging his authority, but I knew filming was starting soon. Clearing my throat, I removed my eyes and turned, seeing Novah and Lia gawking at us both.

"Novah, can you tell Danielle I'll be out soon?" I said, heading back to my seat. Dominic narrowed his brow, shaking his head and walking out.

I released a harsh breath and relaxed my shoulders. Novah and Lia both stared at me curiously.

"What are you two looking at me for?"

"The sexual tension between you two. Girl, just sleep with him and get it over with," Lia replied, fanning herself.

"He's not my type," I stated.

"The attractive, tall, hard muscles, perfect plump lips for eating the soul out of your body type of guy. On top of that, a mature man with a job and no kids," Lia said, running down his traits.

"The arrogant, over the top and wanting to be in control, alpha asshole," I sassed.

CHAPTER SEVEN

Dominic

Emmanuel was ripping on me for going off about what she was wearing. I wouldn't even let my sister wear something like that on a beach. That damn swimsuit was too little for her thick frame. She knew what she was doing when she decided to put it on, and I wasn't about to have all these dudes up here, fawning and drooling at her like she was a piece of meat.

"I think you should admit you have a crush on her and get it over with," Emmanuel stated.

"Everyone check out okay with background checks?" I asked, changing the subject.

"Nice way to tell me to shut up. Everything checked out. The last sample that was sent to the lab was off like the last batch. Danielle wants to meet tomorrow with Elijah to discuss what further steps we need to take," Emmanuel informed me. He'd been by my side for the Jacinda debacle and brought me back to my sanity whenever I went to that dark place and shut people out. I called him my conscience because when I'm ready to kick someone's ass, he's right there pulling me back from the brink. Then, he'll joke on me afterward for losing my cool.

"Only way from what I see," I responded as the door to Lauren's dressing room opened. She stepped out in her bathing suit and shorts, hair swooped to the side with minimal makeup. Her friend, Novah, walked behind her and winked at us. I tipped my head at them as they strolled to the cabana. Danielle spoke to her about the different products she had laid out on the table. I guessed the mixture of drinks, makeup, and friends hanging around us was supposed to sell the lipstick.

"You stare any longer, she's going to think you're interested," Emmanuel joked.

I waved him off, moving in closer to watch, but not enough to distract. The photographer yelled out for everyone to move out of the shot, and I saw she was still wearing the shorts. Lauren looked over her shoulder, and we made eye contact. A few seconds later, she turned away and picked up the lipstick to pose.

"I guess you have some influence," Emmanuel stated.

"You know I wouldn't even let my sister wear some thong bikini. Who even makes shit like that?"

"Beats me. Your girl loves the camera though," he remarked, and I nodded watching as she posed, changing positions flawlessly. Either she was holding the lipstick next to her face, pretending to open the container or pass it to a co-star. She was good at her job, no doubt.

Seven hours later, we wrapped up the shoot, and I waited for Lauren to come out of her dressing room to follow her home.

"Dominic. Great job today, we have some great shots, and the lighting was perfect," Danielle insisted, showing me some of the shots.

"I'm happy for you, Danielle. Next time can we do it under the air conditioner? It was hot as hell out here."

She chuckled at my comment. "I'll make a note of that. Are you still following her home?" she questioned, and I nodded yes.

"These flowers were delivered for her, can you pass them to her? I'll see you tomorrow at the meeting. I'm getting frustrated by links and then someone messing with the formula."

I took the flowers out of her hands. "I agree, it's not just a random one-off situation. Based on everything that keeps popping up, I think it's coming from the inside."

"Well, let's hope we can figure it out soon, D," Danielle replied, before walking off toward her car right as the trailer door opened.

"You're still here?" Novah asked, followed by Lauren wrapped in the clothes she had on earlier, plus shades.

"I wanted to make sure you both got home safe. I'll follow you in your car and Lauren, these came for you."

"Who are they from?" she asked, taking the flowers out of my hands.

I shrugged, not knowing or caring.

"Read the card," I stated, putting up a front. If it was her boyfriend, then he should have been here protecting her—something I would do if she was my woman.

She read the card, and her eyebrows furrowed in confusion. A second later, she balled it up.

"What did the card say?" I questioned.

"Nothing important. I'm ready to go home and soak in the tub."

"Had to be serious enough for you to ball it up. What if your boyfriend ordered the wrong kind?"

"I don't have a boyfriend if you must know. It was just a random congrats note," she said, following Novah to the car.

"Well, I'll follow you two, and then I'll be on my way home."

"No date tonight, Mr. Combs?" Novah asked.

I smirked, shaking my head no. "Not tonight, Novah. I have a full-time job; dating is the last thing on my mind."

"How old are you, if you don't mind me asking?" Novah queried, opening the driver's side door.

"I'm thirty-six."

"The perfect age, not too young to play games and not too old that you'd need Viagra to keep it up," she joked, and I bent over laughing at her statement. Lauren's mouth hung wide open.

"Thanks. Where are you from? Do you model?"

"No, I'm from New York like Lauren. We've been best friends since middle school. I am an accountant and am in the process of starting my own business, and I help Lauren sometimes when she needs me," Novah answered.

Novah was funny as hell, and I liked her personality. She was laidback and cool, unlike her spoiled friend.

"Was she always like this?" I asked.

"Yep." Novah and I busted out in laughter at her statement. Lauren grunted, mumbling under her breath.

"Novah, the last thing I need is him in my business," Lauren said.

"Novah, make sure the princess gets home safely.

Following right behind you guys," I told her and jogged to my car. Emmanuel already left an hour ago with most of the team. It was only me to finish off any last-minute details. Novah honked her horn, and I flicked my lights on and off, letting her know I was ready for her to lead the way. It wasn't too late, so I could make it home in time to cook and finish watching a movie. I sighed. I liked my life simple without interruptions. No longer in the navy, I still went by a regimen from the time I got up until it was time for me to go to bed. As I drove behind Novah, my phone started to ring. I clicked the Bluetooth in my car before answering the call.

"When are you coming home?" Devan questioned.

"Soon, why?" I answered, turning left to get on the freeway.

"I wanted to know if you could bring me something to eat."

That's Devan, my little sister, spoiled and last minute with everything. She waits until the day is half done to say something about being hungry. I had food in my fridge, she was just too lazy to cook.

"Where are you?" I hesitated to ask but knew the answer by the background of the surrounding sound of the speakers.

"Your house," Devan answered.

"Didn't you just move into your own place, little girl?" I fussed.

"I did, but I was bored, and I wanted to hang out with my big brother. Desmond wasn't doing much, and the kids were fighting over the remote, so I left. Please, D, bring me some food," Devan pleaded.

"Devan, there's food in the fridge and I'm exhausted and not going back out for the rest of the night. Hold up. Let me call you back," I said, not waiting for her to reply back. I hung up as we pulled into the parking lot of Lauren's apartment complex. Getting out of my car, I headed to Novah and Lauren to walk them to the door.

"You didn't need to walk us to the door, D," Novah said. I tilted my head in surprise at her calling me D.

"I overheard Danielle calling you that. I hope it's okay?"

"It's cool. You ladies have a good night," I said, starting to walk away.

"Do you want to come in for dinner? I know Lauren was planning on watching some new horror film, which I will probably fall asleep to. But she could use the company." Novah hinted at trying to get Lauren and I alone together. I chuckled at Lauren's eyes, which rose in surprise at her admission.

"Novah! Stop trying to push that boy on me."

"Novah, I'm good, and Lauren?"

"What!" she huffed, sticking her foot in the door, about to walk inside.

"Nothing about me is a boy. Stay safe, princess, and

I'll see you tomorrow," I commented, as I lifted her chin, stared into her eyes, before I winked and headed to my car.

CHAPTER EIGHT

Dominic

Last night, Devan kept me up until two in the morning watching movies. I found out she'd just broken up with her boyfriend and didn't want to be alone. Something all of my siblings and Elias will do. Come over and bug me when something in their lives is wrong. Now, as I sat in the meeting with Danielle and Elijah, doing a video conference with Mark and Zoe discussing the lab's latest findings as well as potential security updates, I realized that I was exhausted.

"So Dominic, do you think we should wait to launch or continue as planned? We have a lot of money wrapped up in advertising from commercials, bill-boards, and social media campaigns," Zoe asked.

"The early numbers show that only one batch with around one hundred containers was tampered with.

We do have the advantage since it hasn't leaked to the media. I believe we can keep it under wraps," I replied.

"But, for how long?" Elijah questioned.

"That I can't answer."

"Should we continue even making more products? Is it worth wasting money?" Danielle inquired, flipping through the photos of lipsticks and foundation bottles with markings of tampered ingredients.

"I think it's something we should consider. I can't tell you how to run your company, Danielle."

"Danielle, if you want to put a pause on things, let me know," Zoe advised.

"Did you watch any surveillance video?" Elijah questioned.

"Emmanuel just installed hidden cameras in the lab. The general videos you have only filmed the entrance and exits. We needed something for every corner in the walls," I replied.

"I hate that it's come to this. I don't want my employees to feel like we're spying on them," Danielle said firmly, tapping her pen on the desk.

"I agree with Danielle. We can't overstep and interrupt the workflow," Elijah commented.

"The cameras are small and were installed at night after the employees left."

"The photoshoot went well, Zoe, we can move forward with everything. I want to have a celebration dinner with everyone to celebrate the campaign. How is the launch party going?" Danielle questioned.

"I have a guest list of a hundred people; I know you wanted it to be intimate. Are we still doing the red carpet?" Zoe inquired.

"D, what do you think?" Danielle asked.

Looking over the information Zoe emailed to us, I scanned through the logistics and nodded my head.

"Emmanuel will contact you, Zoe, to fine-tune some things, I know this is important to Danielle and Raven Cosmetics. Let me have a little time doing a walk through. When is dinner?"

"Tomorrow," Danielle responded.

"Okay, we can revisit after dinner. I need to head out and check in on Lauren."

"How are things with you and Lauren?" Zoe questioned.

I closed my folder and computer, glanced between Danielle and Elijah. "What have you heard about, Zoe?"

She shrugged her shoulders. "I want to hear your version of events."

"Twilight has been talking shit, I see." I stopped mid-stride, eyebrows slanted in a frown.

All three of them cracked up in laughter.

"Shooter, come on. I didn't tell Zoe anything when she sent over the details of what security they need," Mark remarked.

"Leave me out of this," Zoe said, biting her lip to stifle a grin.

"I'll leave you three to talk about my love life behind my back. I have real work to do."

I wandered out of the conference room and headed toward the exit. As I neared the elevator, I saw Lauren in her office. All of the offices had clear glass; nothing could be hidden even if you wanted it to. I checked the time because I thought Emmanuel had told me she'd be working from home today.

Heading in her direction, I tapped on the door, not waiting for her to call me inside.

"First, you don't have elevator etiquette; now you walk into rooms without being invited," Lauren said, standing up from her desk. Admiring her presence caused every hair on my scalp to stand at attention, every skin cell tingled, and warmth spread across my chest. I needed to focus and not let another pretty face fool me.

"I had a meeting down the hall, and I'd planned to go to your place. Emmanuel said you were working from home. Who brought you here?" I questioned, meeting her halfway, sliding my hands in my pockets.

"Novah dropped me off, and I did start working from home, but it was boring, and I wanted to see if I could get some shots of the lab for a few posts. I'm working on something for my fans."

"Did Emmanuel follow you up here?" I inquired.

"Are you always this uptight? All work, never taking a break, Dominic."

Lauren weaved toward her desk and picked up her phone.

"You mean doing my job."

Lauren held her camera up to take a picture, and I blocked it with my hand.

"Stop being so stuffy; one photo won't hurt." She tapped me on the chest. I grasped her palm, the spark between us was felt and we released our hands immediately.

"I move in silence, Lauren, for a reason. The reason Elijah wanted me, in this case, is not only for your safety but for the company as well. Has anything weird happened lately?" I questioned, not forgetting about the flowers someone left at the photoshoot.

"A few text messages, nothing too crazy. I think it's an ex-boyfriend or something," she casually stated.

"Ex-boyfriend. Why didn't you say anything earlier? Give me his name, and I'll look into it and let me see your phone."

"Why?" she asked, holding it away from me.

"I need to get my tech guys to search your phone, and we can trace where the messages are coming from." I reached a hand out to grab the phone, and she held it behind her back. I groaned in frustration, trying to reach around her, and she almost sidestepped out of the way, moving left, and I blocked her movement, and we fell with me on top of her.

“Sorry,” I apologized, out of breath, holding onto her waist.

CHAPTER NINE

Lauren

His lips brushed my ear, raising goosebumps across my skin. I swallowed the lump in my throat. I felt like a girl on a first date. I silently sniffed him, closing my eyes discreetly.

"Did you just sniff me?" he asked.

"Maybe."

"Can I see your phone, Lauren, please?"

I nodded, passing him my phone, not ready for him to get up. This was the closest I'd been to being under a man in about eight months. If I wasn't so annoyed by him, I'd ask if he was dating anyone.

"Can I get up now?" I questioned.

"Yeah, sorry." He jumped up and reached down to help me up. I was glad I wore a pantsuit today.

A knock on the door interrupted the awkward moment.

"Yes, come in." Josslyn walked in with Carol.

"Hi, Dominic, we came to see if Lauren was available to answer some questions with a reporter. This was last minute, and Danielle wanted to see if you wouldn't mind."

"Sure, of course. Let me finish wrapping things up here. Where are they?"

"The conference room," Carol said.

"Okay, perfect, I'll be down in a minute."

Carol waved goodbye as Josslyn stood to wait.

"I wanted to give you the second sample; I know you wanted to practice on a body glow that had a light fragrance. I have three types for you," Josslyn commented.

"Does Danielle know about this?" Dominic questioned, picking up the samples, twirling them around. I snatched them out of his hands.

"Of course, she does, it was her idea. Can I have my phone back, so I can go?"

He opened my phone and typed something, pulling his phone out as well.

"What are you doing?" I asked.

"Taking your number down and programming mine in, just in case you need me."

"I have Emmanuel's number," I said.

Dominic handed my phone back. "Now, you have mine. I'm heading out to run a few errands. Call me when you're ready to leave for the day," he said and walked out.

"He seems friendly."

"Josslyn, the man is aggravating. Come on, let's go to the conference room."

I locked up my office, chatting with Jossyln about the ideas for the launch party. We entered the conference room, and I noticed a woman sitting down, talking on her phone. She smiled, then held up her hand, waving at me to wait a minute.

"Do you need me to stay?" Josslyn asked.

"No. I'll be fine."

Josslyn strolled out, closing the door, and I sat down at the conference table, waiting for her to finish.

"OMG. So sorry, Lauren, I can't believe how busy it gets when the news cycle is all about who's dating who. I'm Jacinda, the reporter for *Maven* magazine. We report on everything from fashion, music, film, celebrities, and more."

"I've heard of you guys. Some articles have gone a little overboard, but for the most part, I read your work."

"Cute. How old are you?" she questioned.

"Why do you ask?"

"No reason. I wanted to speak with you for a few minutes about your work with Raven Cosmetics, and what's in store for you next."

"We started a few weeks ago, and things are

running smoothly. Danielle, the CEO, listens to me and takes my opinions in with certain discussion promo or design aspects," I replied. She took notes and recorded our conversation.

"That's great; I know most companies pay you a check and expect you to just smile and post."

"Danielle is different, and it's one of the reasons I signed with them. Did you get a chance to talk with her?"

"No, she was busy when I came and couldn't talk. How has your fame been affected since you've blown up even more?"

"I'm still the same Lauren Armstrong from New York and I'm still humble. My parents weren't on board, but slowly over time, I know they'll come around. My brother loves the limelight."

"What about your boyfriend, Raymond?" she questioned.

"My ex-boyfriend."

"According to him, you guys broke up because you recorded a sex tape and stole money from him," she said, looking through her notes. I jumped out of my seat.

"What! That's a lie."

"I'm sorry, Lauren, I have it on record here."

"What sex tape? Raymond is a no-good bum."

"Giving you the heads up, my magazine is going to run the story soon. You probably want to get ahead of it before it becomes a huge problem," Jacinda said, standing up, grabbing her notepad and tape recorder.

Storming out of the office, looking around for Danielle, I bumped into Ben.

"Woah, is everything okay?" Ben asked. When he let my arms go, I began pacing back and forth, my anger steadily rising.

"That son of a bitch!" I screamed.

Carol walked down the hall talking with Josslyn and from the look of things, an argument was brewing there, but right now, all I could think about was what I was just told.

"Lauren, are you all right? I saw you looked upset running out of the conference room. Who was that woman?" Carol questioned.

"Some woman from a magazine. Josslyn, did she tell you what she wanted to talk to me about?"

"She didn't, sorry, what happened?" Josslyn queried.

"It wasn't a pleasant interview. She's basically trying to publish some bullshit piece about me and my ex."

"I can't believe that. She really made it seem like she wanted to do a girl power type of day in your life article," Josslyn replied.

"Yeah that didn't happen. I need to go."

CHAPTER TEN

Lauren

Raymond was acting like he was some perfect boyfriend. Before the article came out, I needed to let Danielle know what was going on to see if we had to do any damage control. I walked toward her office, only to see her walking out with her bag, talking with her assistant.

"Danielle, can I talk to you?" I asked.

"I was leaving for the day; can you walk with me? Kimberly, can you send out the invitations for dinner? Ben, did you need something?" Danielle asked.

"No, I was checking on Lauren, she seemed upset," Ben said with his hand on the lower part of my back. I stepped out of his hold, and he smiled, striding off.

"What's wrong, Lauren? You look like you... you just saw a ghost."

"Feels like it, my ex-boyfriend Raymond spoke with

some tabloid magazine. Used to be a magazine I read, now I'm for sure canceling my subscription. She said Raymond accused me of making a sex tape," I rushed out, biting my nails, thinking back on a time I told him to record us.

"What magazine? They were here?" Danielle questioned.

"*Maven* magazine. Some woman named Jackie, no Joyce...shit, I forget."

"Okay, calm down. Go home and relax. We have the dinner tomorrow and we have a lot to celebrate. I'll call Zoe and find out if she knows anything. Don't stress yourself out."

"Easy for you to say, your ex isn't trying to take you down before your career even starts," I told her, stepping on the elevator with her.

"I've seen my share of drama with my friends; this will blow over in a day or two," Danielle said, hitting the L for the lobby.

As soon as the elevator dinged, I pulled out my phone to call Dominic to pick me up, unfortunately before I could, I was surprised by some unexpected guests.

"Surprise!" my family screamed, running toward me, as Danielle stood off to the side, giggling at my fake smile.

"I'll see you tomorrow, Lauren," Danielle stated.

I waved goodbye, thinking about how I was going

to juggle my family visiting unannounced on top of everything else in my life.

"Are you surprised to see us, pudding?" my dad asked, kissing my forehead.

To Kenny Armstrong, I'd always be his pudding. He made sure everyone knew, and I used to get embarrassed growing up, but now, I'm fine with him keeping that image of me being someone he will always protect.

"I am, Pops, when did you guys get in?" I inquired, taking the bag out of my mom's arm.

"This morning. We checked into a hotel and relaxed before coming here to see you. We talked to Novah, and she gave us the address."

"Isn't that sweet of Novah," I said, rolling my eyes, pushing the door open. Hearing a car honk, I looked up and saw Dominic in a black Lexus SUV, waiting.

"I was just about to call you."

"A part of me felt you wouldn't, so I finished up my errands earlier and came back. Mr. and Mrs. Armstrong, nice to meet you," he said, extending his hand to my father and mother. Kenny Jr. shook hands with him.

"No reason for me to ask how you know them. Being the military bodyguard, you probably have the CIA on speed dial," I joked, opening the back door of the car for my brother to get inside.

"CIA, FBI, and a few prime ministers," Dominic

answered, opening the door for me to get in on the passenger side.

"Thanks," I said, watching him jog over to the driver's side before I leaned over to unlock the door.

"What's your name again, son?" my mom asked.

"Dominic Combs, Ma'am."

"Are you married?"

"Ma!"

"What? It never hurts to ask."

"Vivien, leave that girl alone," Kenny Sr. said.

Dominic drove us to their hotel, and I stayed with them through dinner until I received a call from Carol about a new discovery she found. I told my parents I would be back later tonight. I jumped up excited to get back to work. I knew she was taking some of my ideas and experimenting and I told her the second something looked good to let me know. I took an Uber since it wouldn't take me long to get there. I didn't think I needed to call Emmanuel and bother him.

"Thanks for the ride," I told the Uber driver and shut the door. Novah was having too much fun with my family, so sliding out was easy.

Showing my badge, I walked through security and waved to Axel, the night security guard.

I knocked on Carol's door, but she didn't hear me, so I knocked again and the door swung open.

"Sorry to bug you so late," Carol said.

"You're not bothering me, my parents understood."

"Awesome! Well I wanted to show you what I've been working on."

She headed to the lab and I fell behind. Placing her badge against the security sign, I followed in and grabbed a lab coat and goggles. Carol opened the glass case that held the samples of colors and gestured for me to take a seat.

"These look good, Carol."

"Well, it's because of your ideas and my science brain that we've come up with the right mixture."

All of the colors looked bold, rich, and smooth. Sliding on gloves, she passed me a test strip to test it out on my arm.

"How many colors are you thinking for the first batch?" I questioned.

"Ultimately, it's up to Danielle, but I think starting with five main colors for a palette would be perfect. Maybe even showing off each one in a different theme."

"These look really good. I can't wait to get these out to my fans."

"I commend you with opening up your life to the public. I doubt I could ever do that," Carol said.

"It's not really too bad. I do have boundaries, but overall they respect me and don't pry."

Shutting the glass case closed, I removed the gloves and followed her over to the desk and we looked at the monitor of all the colors up close together. She pointed toward a light pink color that looked like cotton candy.

"I know you guys have the signature red look but think about this pink possibly being added to the collection," she said. I nodded taking in all of her details and keeping notes on what worked and what didn't.

"Danielle has a vision for the launch, we can always present these to her for the second launch."

"It's getting late, I need to get home to my husband and kids. We can talk more tomorrow," Carol informed me, removing her coat and grabbing her jacket and purse.

"How long have you been married?"

"Too long, and these kids drive me crazy. Take my advice, stay single as long as you can," Carol joked.

I chuckled and followed behind her calling for an Uber to go back to the hotel.

CHAPTER ELEVEN

Dominic

My office was in the process of being upgraded, so I sat in Emmanuel's office with him going over the product line dates of when things started to get tampered with. I opened my laptop and looked through the video footage from yesterday. Seeing Josslyn and Carol talking in the lab and changing out containers, nothing looked off. All of the employees went through interviews and background checks.

"Gentlemen, I see you're stuck in the middle of surveillance. Any leads I can give Danielle?" Elijah questioned, strolling inside with Mark.

"We had our guys going through hours of footage and narrowed it down to the prime hours of late afternoon and early morning when packages are sent for testing. That places most of your lab team that works around those hours as potential suspects."

"That would be about five total people. Carol's the lead manager; I doubt she would do anything like this. She's been with the company since it started," Elijah responded.

"I was thinking the same thing, and she's much older and probably has a pension and family to take care of so she wouldn't get involved in something like this," I said.

"Well, keep me updated, and how have you been overall?" Elijah asked.

"Are you asking as a friend or owner of Raven Cosmetics?" I answered.

"Both."

"He has a crush on Lauren and refuses to act on it," Emmanuel teased.

"She's too young, immature, self-involved, and probably like my ex, money hungry."

"I didn't hear you say no to his questions, though. Maybe it's time that you started dating again," Mark suggested.

"Coming from the married guy. Why are all my friends trying to get me to marry and settle down?"

"Married life has its perks. Let's not bring up Jacinda, makes my skin crawl," Mark joked.

"Have you heard from Jacinda? It's been three or four years, right?" Emmanuel asked.

"The last time I heard she was working for some magazine, not sure if she's still there. I tend to keep our circles separate after everything that went down with trying to pin a baby on me. Had me thinking I was going to be a father all that time, and she was sleeping with someone else," I told the two of them, going over in my head the last relationship that caused my heart to harden at the idea of being with another woman being physically released.

"It didn't help that we were dealing with Jackson being shot at the time," Mark mentioned.

"Let's get out of here and head to dinner, I'm starving and ready to meet your in-laws. I heard Kenny Sr. is just as tall as you," Mark joked, curving away from my left hook and heading out. I closed the file folders, Emmanuel grabbed his jacket, and I followed behind. Danielle had put together this dinner at some exclusive restaurant and we had no choice but to go.

Forty-five minutes later, we arrived across town in separate cars. I rode with Mark and Emmanuel trailed behind in his car since he lived farther away than Mark. We stepped out of the cars and already noticed photographers hanging outside.

"The restaurant is closed for the night, right? Did someone tip off the photographers that we'd be here?" I queried, pushing the photographers to get inside.

"Hey man! Almost knocked me down," the photographer yelled, picking up his hat off the ground.

"Get a real job," I remarked back, ready to throw his camera in the trash.

Mark chuckled, and I waved him off, not caring how I looked. I hated how people constantly pried into other people's business. Diablo's was down the street from Lynnhaven Fish House, where we normally hung out for lunch with my boys.

Everyone was already seated when we arrived except for Lauren. I glanced around the room, ready to shut the place down if something had happened to her.

"Where's Lauren?" I asked Danielle as she passed the wine menu around the table.

"She stepped into the ladies' room. You look like your normal self today. I know the boys get on you about constantly wearing your suits, and now everyone's in suits."

I nodded and caught Lauren out of the corner of my eye walking back with a harsh glare on her face. I was completely caught off guard with the curve of her hips in a tight-fitting, long black dress that went up to her neck, with her hair pulled up away from her face. She looked like an angel, someone that I needed to try and stay away from. Automatically, I pulled the chair out next to me for her to sit. It was the opposite of how she looked at the beach, a totally different person.

"I didn't think this was your type of thing,

Dominic," Lauren said, picking up her napkin, laying it across her lap.

"I go wherever my client needs me to go," I replied.

"After dinner, we can talk. I want to apologize for how we met and then the dust-up at the beach."

"What upset you when you came from the bathroom?"

"What are you talking about?"

"You looked upset, your face had a frown on it, and I'm not used to you frowning. More like posing for the camera every five minutes."

"Ohh, nothing, but my ex-boyfriend."

"What did he do?"

"He's claiming I have a sex tape," she said calmly.

"I've seen it and it's going to sell a lot of magazines." The entire table glanced up at the voice that I knew all too well.

"What are you doing here?" Lauren jumped up, ready to fight Jacinda.

I was shocked at the two possibly knowing each other. Lauren almost yanked away from me.

"Jacinda, what are you doing here?" I asked, causing Lauren to glare at me.

"How do you know that bitch?" Lauren questioned.

"Dominic, I didn't know you were working with Raven Cosmetics. Long time, maybe we can do dinner and catch up like old friends," Jacinda wondered out loud.

"Let me go!" Lauren shouted. Her mom tried to help me calm her down to no avail.

"Jacinda, what are you doing here? This is a private dinner," Danielle stated.

"I'm running a story on your tainted makeup line and wanted to get an exclusive from you first. I wanted to give you the first opportunity to talk about what's happening. The minute this hits the news cycle, your company will end up very much in the bottom of the barrel, Danielle," Jacinda snidely commented.

"Danielle, she's the one that came to the office the other day and did the interview with me," Lauren advised.

"Wait, she was at Raven? What time?" Danielle asked.

"Sometime after you left when Josslyn and Carol came to my office," Lauren said, pointing to them at the table.

"Lauren, who gave her permission to interview you?" Danielle questioned, peering at Elijah and Zoe.

"Josslyn told me she was confirmed through you," Lauren stated.

"Josslyn, I never set up an interview with a magazine. Carol, do you know anything about this because Zoe is the PR and would have sent word ahead of time?" Danielle argued.

"This is the first I've heard of this, Danielle. Josslyn, do you know this woman?" Carol pointed at

Jacinda. My eyes narrowed in frustration. For her to get so close to Lauren and I didn't know about it was pissing me off.

Josslyn shook her head no, and Lauren's mouth dropped open in surprise.

"Wait, am I on candid camera or something? Josslyn, you introduced me to her," Lauren mentioned, and I believed her. Something about Josslyn was on my radar; she stood off when everyone else talked, or had a way of blending in the background, knowing the cameras were watching at certain times. I remembered a few days ago she needed to stay late from what Emmanuel told me because she needed to get some notes documented for the launch.

"Listen, Lauren, if you want to call me and give me an interview, I would be willing to sit with you, but the timeline is only for twenty-four hours. Danielle, I'll be in touch. Dominic, it was nice seeing you again. I hope we can talk and clear the air," Jacinda said, picking up a glass of wine off the table and taking a sip. She smiled, walking away as everyone sat shocked at what transpired.

I ran a hand up and down Lauren's back. I could tell she was getting angry with the silence from Josslyn. I would need to get my team on top of this breach asap because Jacinda was known as being underhanded and evil when she wanted something. Her showing up at Raven wasn't just to get an interview with Lauren.

I'd have my men look into her again because I didn't know the woman I was looking at just a few minutes ago. Lauren stomped off and Danielle started to get up and follow behind her. I held my hand up for her to stop.

"Let me talk with her."

"Are you sure? She comes off strong, but Lauren's really vulnerable and not as tough as she seems," Danielle replied.

"I'm the best person that knows anything about not being really strong underneath and tough on the outside. Losing my brothers in Iraq crosses my mind every day, Danielle."

She patted me on the shoulder, and I headed to check on Lauren.

She was pacing back and forth near the exit.

I reached out and grabbed her arm, turning her to face me.

"Hey, you good?"

"Yeah, sorry for walking off."

"No worries, it happens. Don't worry about Jacinda, I'll have my men check over the tapes."

"I can't have anyone trying to destroy what I'm building, Dominic," she softly said, burying her head in my chest. I rubbed her back, hoping to calm her down.

"I got you, princess."

"That's old, man," she joked as she wiped the tears pooling in her eyes.

CHAPTER TWELVE

Dominic

One week later...

It was all over the news that Raven Cosmetics had tainted makeup that caused a few people to scar. The publicity wasn't helping Lauren either, and she stayed holed up in her condo. Her family was getting ready to leave in a few days and wanted her to try and come back to New York for a few days. I parked my car and got out. After talking with Danielle, we were speeding up the investigation and retraining everyone that worked in the lab, even limiting the amount of people that handled the product. Carol had to reassign Josslyn until further notice because of the magazine screw-up. She denied knowing what type of magazine Jacinda worked for but did confess to introducing Lauren to her at the office.

Grabbing the bag of takeout from my mom's home and several movies, I tapped the doorbell waiting for someone to answer. A few seconds later, the door opened with Lauren only wearing a crop top with no bra and boy shorts.

"It's the middle of the day, Dominic, why are you here?"

"I came to talk and maybe get you out of the house." I didn't wait for the invitation and stepped inside, moving over so she could shut the door. I followed her toward the kitchen and admired her loft.

"You have a nice place."

"Thanks, Novah helped me decorate."

"How many rooms, if you don't mind me asking?" I placed the bags on the kitchen counter. It sat away from the living room with an open archway and a counter for guests to sit at the bar and still communicate.

"Three bedrooms and two baths," she replied, grabbing the plates out of the cabinet.

"I hope you're hungry, my mom cooked a lot of food, and I knew I wouldn't be able to finish everything."

"I can eat a little something, but I'm watching my diet," Lauren answered.

"You're kidding, right?"

"No, I've gained weight since I moved out here. My ass is huge now."

She turned around, showing me her butt, and I licked my lips, wishing under different circumstances I didn't think she was too complicated. I could see us hanging out.

"Your ass looks fine to me," I told her, winking and passing the box of yams and lasagna.

"Momma cooked for an entire football team. I can't eat all of that, Dominic."

"Try for me, and I'll give you something in return."

She rolled her eyes and went to sit down on the couch. I picked up my plate and sat down next to her, passing the movie I picked out.

"*Lethal Weapon*," Lauren said.

"Why not? It's a classic, but you're probably too young to understand the dynamics of the buddy cop movies."

"I'm twenty-five, Dominic, not eighteen. I can teach you a few things, probably. This is the first time I've seen you actually smile, and you're wearing regular jeans and a shirt. Thank God you didn't drive over here in a double-breasted suit and tie. I would probably have to pretend I didn't know you," Lauren joked. I nudged her in the side playfully.

"And I'm thirty-six, which means I get the first pick of the movie."

"OMG! You're such a big baby. For someone that's

older than me, you probably think I can't kick your ass."

"I know you can't. Navy, baby, you can't touch this," I said, showing off my muscles under my t-shirt.

"Boy please, those little muscles aren't fooling anybody," she said, putting her plate on the table, challenging me to arm wrestling.

Shaking my head, I put my plate down and sat around on the opposite end of the table with my arm up, ready to battle.

"How do we do this? Best two out of three or just one round and shake on it?" I questioned.

"One round and shake on it, and if I win, you have to do whatever I say for one day."

"What do I get if I win?"

"I won't question you back when you need me to do something, especially on-location at a shoot."

"Let's shake on it," I said and extended a hand. She placed her hand in mine, and we agreed.

"On the count of three. May the best person win," Lauren replied.

"Agree."

"One, Two. Three." We both spoke at the same time, and she was way more durable than I thought, but I knew I had it in the bag until she lifted her shirt, and I lost my concentration, and she slammed my hand down, jumping up, yelling I won.

"Hold up! You cheated."

She started dancing around the room and ran over to the window, yelling out, “I won! I won!”

“Lauren, you cheated,” I fussed, and she sauntered over chuckling, clapping her hands together.

“I never said how I would win.” The smile in her eyes maintained a sensual flame. Lauren pushed me in the chest gently, winking.

Grasping her hand, I pulled her down on the couch, caressing her cheek.

“Based on you cheating to win, princess.”

CHAPTER THIRTEEN

Lauren

My whole being seemed to be filled with waiting. Slowly, his gaze raked over me, and I licked my lips in silent expectation. His nearness made my senses spin. It was too easy to get caught in the way he looked at me. I wasn't sure if he felt the same way about what should happen next, but I needed to know if this was just a one-sided attraction. I had no desire to back away from his touch. I leaned up closer, giving myself freely to his kiss.

"What are you doing?" he whispered, peering into my eyes.

"Claiming my prize, I want you to kiss me, Dominic," I said, gripping his shirt.

"This isn't a good idea," he said, brushing his lips against mine.

The strong hardness of his lips against mine had

me wanting him to explore the recesses of my mouth. His tongue demanded entry, and I was shocked at my own eager response to his touch. He wrapped his arms around my waist, pulling me in closer.

"What are we doing, Lauren?" he asked, showering kisses around my lips, along my jaw and shoulder.

"Two adults that find each other attractive, giving in to pleasure," I told him, leaving his mouth, taking control of what we both wanted. Straddling his lap, I helped him remove his shirt, and he did the same with me. His eyes stared into mine, asking for permission.

"I want this, Dominic, and I won't regret what happens. Even if we never speak of this again."

"I didn't come here for this," he said, running his hand up and down my back.

He fondled my breasts. My head fell back, quivering at his touch as his lips captured my nipple.

"Blame it on me winning," I moaned, cupping the back of his neck, pushing him further in my chest. His tongue ran across my nipples and I found myself begging for his caress. I gripped the back of his neck, down to his chest, journeying toward his hard erection. Biting my lip, I spread my thighs even more, against all logic, I melted against him.

"You're trouble, Lauren. What am I going to do with you?" he groaned, trailing kisses up the middle of my neck. Wrapping his hand, he gently squeezed, forcing me to stare into his eyes for confirmation that we were really doing this.

He probably thought I would be one of those women that couldn't handle one-night stands after the weeks and months of craziness in my life. I needed to be Lauren and not the social media celebrity, the daughter of Vivien and Kenny, or even a girl that needed a commitment from a relationship.

"Whatever you want to do."

"Then we need to take this to the bedroom. I'm a big man, and this little ass couch won't do."

He lifted us off the couch, and I wrapped my legs around him, my nails digging into his shoulders as I arched toward his kiss. "Which room?" he questioned, continuing the kiss.

"The first one to the left," I answered. He squeezed my ass and kicked the door open. He dropped me down on the bed, then removed his pants.

"Do you have condoms?" I asked, in case I needed to grab one out of my dresser drawer. Novah would be gone for hours today. I hoped he had enough energy to last all night.

Dominic slid his hands in his pants, pulled out his wallet, grabbed two condoms, and tossed them on the bed.

"Remove your shorts and open your legs. I'm ready to find out if your bite is as good as your bark." Dominic bent down, brushed his hand against my swollen folds while I bit my nails. I opened my thighs even more. His tongue raked over my sex with one smooth, slick glide.

"Shit..." I cried out, closing my legs around his head.

My heart pounded an erratic rhythm at his touch.

"Mhmmm...Give me what you have."

A quiver surged through my veins, arched into the intrusion of his finger. "Ahhh!! Domi...nic...," I stuttered. I was clenching the sheets, tossing my head to the side. A knot rose in my throat, and I tried to push him away.

"I can't take it anymore," I said, out of breath.

He chuckled at my statement. "What happened to you being able to handle anything? You're grown, right?" I stuck my middle finger up, grabbing the pillow to put between my legs. I was ready to fall asleep, and he was pissing me off. He started kissing my back, down to my ass, spreading my legs hungry for more and sticking his tongue inside my ass. I jumped slightly. None of my exes ever wanted to explore anything from the back. This feeling was different, but not bad.

"Oohhh, Dominic...Shit! Keep going." I reached over to hold onto the headboard as his tongue fucked me at a slow pace. Slapping my ass, he abruptly stopped. I looked over my shoulder and saw him grab the condom, stroking himself and putting it on. I tried to turn around. He shook his head no. Lifting my leg, he slid inside my sex, and I almost couldn't breathe. His girth had to be never-ending because I felt him in my stomach.

"Damn, you feel good, princess."

"You're too big. Ahhh...wait, Dominic!" I shouted, wanting to kick myself in the ass for cheating and having to hear him brag about me not being able to handle him in bed.

"Wait for what, baby? Huh. You were talking all that shit. Show me what you can do," he commented back, easing out of me, laying down on his back, smirking.

"Fuck you...old man."

"That's what I'm trying to do, but you can't hang, baby." He chuckled.

Taking in a sharp breath, I rested a hand on his dick before I straddled his lap and slid on top of his erection. Licking my lips, I placed both feet flat on the bed, preparing to ride him until we both came. He thrust his pelvis up. We entwined our hands rocking in unison as his chest rose and fell in rapid breaths.

"Just like that," Dominic said.

"Yes, baby."

Our bodies slapped together, while grunts and moans enveloped the room. He grasped my breast, licked his left hand, and played with my clit.

"Laurennn!!! Ugh...God Damn. Keep going, baby; your pussy is squeezing my dick."

"Mmmmm...Dominic, come with me," I cried out, rocking harder back and forth. We made eye contact, and something shifted in my soul. Not being able to explain it, I bent down to kiss him as my body shuddered from the orgasm. I fell on top of him, unmoving. He wrapped his arms around me, rubbed my back, and kissed my forehead as our bodies drifted off to sleep.

CHAPTER FOURTEEN

Lauren

"Wake up, sunshine. I made breakfast," Novah yelled from the other side of the door. I heard a knock but had no desire to move.

"Novah, leave me alone," I shouted, feeling Dominic pull me closer to his chest, kissing the back of my head.

"You two need to get up. It's almost nine in the morning. Danielle called the house phone looking for you," Novah replied back. We both groaned. We'd been hearing our phones go off throughout the morning; neither of us moved to answer.

"She's right, and I need to head out," Dominic spoke, removing his arms and sitting up in bed. I looked over my shoulder, noticing a tattoo on his back with the name Frogmen.

"Why do you have a tattoo named Frogmen on

your back?" I asked, sitting up, drawing the sheet to cover my breasts. He picked up his phone and began scrolling through his messages; a deep frown marred his face.

"Check your phone," he said.

"What's wrong?" I asked as I looked for my phone, then picked it up off the charger.

"A name for my SEAL team from the Navy. Danielle text you 911 on your phone?" he asked, standing up and grabbing his pants off the floor.

"WTF!" I screamed, clicking on a message that went to an article on *Maven* magazine stating that Raven Cosmetics had damaging products, but the top celebrity influencer had a sex tape that would draw the line for families.

"Who is this bitch?" I yelled to myself, jumping out of bed.

"My ex," Dominic responded as I started getting dressed.

"You didn't think to tell me that at dinner? She's out to destroy Raven Cosmetics and me."

"I broke up with her because she cheated, lied, and tried to pin a baby on me. My past ain't pretty when it comes to the dating department, Lauren. Aren't you the one dealing with a sex tape? We both have crazy exes," he told me.

"I need to shower and head into the office," I said, walking off toward the bathroom.

"Fine, I'll have Emmanuel drive you. Hey!"

"What?"

"We need to talk about what happened yesterday. Once things cool down."

"Yeah," I said, not waiting for him to continue.

An hour later, I was walking through Danielle's office where Elijah, Zoe, Dominic, and Emmanuel were sitting around talking. She looked upset and annoyed. I was worried that they were probably ready to fire me over this.

"Danielle, I'm so sorry-" I started to say but she held her hand up, stopping me.

"It's not your fault. I underestimated Jacinda, and now she's trying to destroy what we've built over the years," Danielle said, reaching out to give me a hug.

"She's your ex-girlfriend. What's the motivation behind bringing Raven Cosmetics down?" Elijah asked.

"I don't know, but I intend to find out," Dominic replied.

"Let me go with you, D. Obviously, she has it bad for destroying this company. Is there anything else we need to know about? I'm calling our lawyer to get the magazine to pull the plug on this story," Danielle stated. I cleared my throat; everyone looked over at me.

"I didn't think this was a big deal at the time, and I thought it was my ex. But I've been receiving text messages from unknown numbers."

"What did the messages say?" Zoe questioned, pulling out her phone.

"Basic stuff- congrats from your number one fan. I think the other was about the photoshoot. I don't remember."

"Anything else?" Dominic asked, jumping out of his seat, walking toward me and placing his hand on my lower back.

"The card from the flowers I got at the beach only said *Will Meet Soon*, and I tossed it in the trash when I left. I wasn't thinking it could be connected to this," I told him.

He caressed my back, and I leaned into him. Everyone stared at us.

"I told Adam to send a cease and desist letter. Don't worry, Lauren, you're not getting fired. We've been your age once; go home and wait for me to call. Zoe, have the party invitations gone out?"

"Yes, we have about a hundred and twenty people coming, and the media has been vetted. So don't stress, Lauren. The show is going on, and this Jacinda person will find out what I do best, and that's putting companies on the map. Raven Cosmetics isn't going anywhere," Zoe announced.

Danielle and Zoe walked out of the office. Dominic nodded to Emmanuel.

“I want Emmanuel to take you home and do a sweep of your place. I’ll be there as soon as I’m done here. We still need to talk,” Dominic stated, lifting my chin and staring into my eyes. I nodded and left with Emmanuel.

CHAPTER FIFTEEN

Dominic

Thirty minutes later we stormed the offices of *Maven* magazine, and I was fucking pissed. The fact that she would stoop this low to destroy someone because they didn't want to do an interview was absolutely ridiculous. Danielle talked with the receptionist, and she wasn't letting us go back, and I didn't care. I charged through the employee entrance, and they followed behind. Knocking and opening door after door, I finally found Jacinda in her office. The secretary tried to jump in front of us to block our entry.

"Tammy, it's okay. I can handle them," Jacinda stated, waving us inside.

"Have you lost your mind? Post a retraction and apologize and remove the link to that fake sex tape of Lauren right now," I demanded. She didn't flinch at my harsh glare. Jacinda crossed her arms, glaring into my eyes.

"No, I did my job. Hello, Danielle and Zoe. Are you here to do an interview?" she questioned.

"Jacinda, you misrepresented yourself and snuck into Raven's to do an interview that wasn't vetted. I expect you to get on the phone and retract every word in that bogus report," Zoe said, picking up the phone.

"My report isn't bogus. I have samples from the company, and we tested it ourselves. Consumers need to know what they are spending their money on. You should be thanking me," Jacinda said, taking a seat behind her desk.

"Let me talk to Jacinda alone for a minute," I suggested.

Zoe and Danielle nodded and stood outside the door.

"I knew you would come around," Jacinda said, licking her lips.

"There will never be you and me again. You fucked that up when you cheated on me."

"I apologized to you about that Dominic, how long are you going to hold onto the past?" Jacinda shouted, jumping out of her seat.

"Forever! I gave you everything, and you threw my heart away and stomped all over it. To top it off, have a kid and pretend he was mine. If I brought an outside child into our relationship after cheating..."

"I would have tried to make it work."

"And yet you still were seeing the guy that you cheated with—all you wanted was my money and status. You never loved me, Jacinda, and pushed away other women because of your deceitful actions."

"What can I do to change your mind?"

"Nothing you do will change my mind but do your job or face the consequences."

"Are you threatening me, Dominic?"

"Yes."

"So, you're trying to save your little girlfriend from public embarrassment. I get it but look at the other women that became even more famous from a sex tape. I'm helping her career actually," she joked.

A knock on the door caused me to turn my head where I saw Danielle peeking in. "Dominic, we should go, I just heard from Adam. We're moving forward with a lawsuit. Don't waste your time trying to appeal to her conscience," Danielle stated.

Jacinda stood up, stalking toward Danielle; I stood blocking her from trying to do anything.

"Don't worry, I'm not going to hurt your boss. Listen, Danielle, I'll give you a little advice, and you can thank me later." Jacinda giggled.

"What is it, Jacinda? Spit it out!" Danielle snapped.

"Has everyone really been loyal at Raven Cosmetics?"

"What does that mean?" Danielle asked.

Jacinda shrugged. "It means the closest one to you could be a far worse enemy than me."

"She's lying. Distracting from the real issue with that fake story," Zoe stated.

"Raven Cosmetics' attorney will be in touch and Jacinda, I suggest you lawyer up. The lawyer for the newspaper already stated they wouldn't back you after hearing Jackson Cole's name being mentioned," Danielle spat.

Zoe and Danielle walked out, and I studied Jacinda's reaction. She smirked, walking back to sit down at her desk and picking up the phone. I wondered if she was contacting Lauren's ex-boyfriend or the leak at Raven. Shaking my head, I turned, pulling my phone out, calling Emmanuel as I walked out of the door to catch up with Zoe and Danielle.

"Yeah," Emmanuel answered, out of breath.

"What are you doing?" I asked, switching the phone from one ear to the next, looking for a notepad in my pocket.

"I just had to chase a photographer from Lauren's place. There were two or three hanging out when we pulled up. She's home now; a little shaken up, but fine."

"Damn, I was hoping it wasn't that close. All right, put a trace on Jacinda's phone and car. I want to know everything she does and who she's talking with. Tell

Lauren I'm on my way now," I said, hanging up the phone.

"You think she took the warning?" Danielle questioned, hopping in the car.

"Only time will tell. Keep the pressure up and monitoring at the lab ramps up. I need eyes on every person that walks in and leaves, including the janitor."

Sliding the key in the ignition, I drove off, heading back to Lauren's place after I dropped Danielle and Zoe off.

"Should we call Jackson and give him a heads up?" Zoe queried.

"Keep Muff out of this until it's absolutely necessary. He's been through enough, and the good thing about all this is that Jacinda tipped her hand."

"What do you mean? The story is out, and social media is having a field day. All day, we've seen posts about the lipstick and body glow line being tainted and not safe," Danielle fussed, leaning her head back on the seat.

"I'm the last person to tell you to stay off social media. But in this situation, we can use it to our advantage. Give the people what they want and direct the focus and turn a negative into a positive."

"How do we do that?" Danielle asked.

"He's right, Danielle, get Lauren and a few people at Raven to handle the social media account to do a Question and Answer. Find out what they're looking for in makeup, push the launch party. Continue spreading that it's only a limited supply that was messed up," Zoe suggested, writing down notes.

"You really think this could work?" Danielle queried, locking eyes with Zoe in the front seat.

"I've made the biggest issues disappear with a little spin. Let me work with Lauren, maybe have her work from a Raven Cosmetics social media account and announce her favorite items are coming out. We drown out the noise of Maven magazine by giving them more of Lauren's personality," Zoe replied.

"I don't want her doing any more photoshoots. We can barely cover the paparazzi hounding her at her place. I can imagine they've swarmed the Raven building," I said, driving down the highway. I checked out the side mirror and saw someone hanging out the window taking photos of my car.

"Damn it!" I shouted, hitting the dashboard.

Zoe and Danielle jumped at the noise.

"What's wrong?"

"Two cars behind us, a photographer was taking shots. Jacinda might have tipped them off," I commented.

Danielle glanced over her shoulder. Zoe pulled out her phone, texting nonstop.

"Mark said he could send backup if we need it," Zoe said.

Shaking my head no, I turned off on the exit

toward the office building. At some point, I knew this would happen. The media hype, public interest, and everyone having an opinion had finally come to a head.

"We'll be fine, have him open the gate so we can get inside and I can drop you both off. Then, I'm heading to see Lauren."

"Tell her to call me," Zoe said as the car stopped in front of the gate a few minutes later. I saw the guard wave us inside. Driving up, I noticed a few Cole Security employees standing around.

"I will."

Danielle and Zoe got out of the car. Mark walked around to the driver's side.

"The whole thing sounds fishy. Emmanuel told me what happened at Lauren's. Make sure you don't kill anyone when you get there. I know you have feelings for her," Mark told me, tapping me on the shoulder.

"She's a client; I want everyone safe. You'd do the same," I replied.

Mark tilted his head. "So, you two haven't slept together?" he asked.

"Time for me to get going. I'll keep you updated and tell Jackson to not come. I know he wants to help, but I got it under control," I said, backing up, driving around him, leaving out of the back entrance to keep photographers from following me. Mark questioning me about Lauren was something I wasn't ready for. Was the connection strong? Yes. Was the sex insane and did it make me crave her even more? Again, yes. The rational part of me knows she's my client, and I never get involved with clients. So why was I so ready to kill Jacinda back at her office for even mentioning Lauren's name? Finally pulling up to her place, I hopped out and walked over to Emmanuel in his car, and he stepped out to shake my hand.

"How is she?"

"She's in her room, not wanting to be bothered. I chased them away, they kept talking about the sex tape, and I don't think it's her," Emmanuel said.

I was caught off guard at his statement. Emmanuel was one of my closest friends, and if he saw Lauren naked, I'd be pissed. I know I didn't have any claims to her, but the feeling of keeping her protected at all costs ran deep in my blood.

"Calm down, before you go off and try to beat my ass. Screenshots are circulating. I didn't see the full thing. Go upstairs and see your girl. Maybe that'll relax you," Emmanuel suggested, reaching out to shake my hand.

CHAPTER SIXTEEN

Lauren

I heard the door opening and didn't feel like even moving to check who it was. Having the covers over my head while locked in my room helped to keep the noise out. Today should have been the day I would prepare to announce the line of cosmetics I collaborated on as well as my exclusive clothing partnership that Danielle was looking to branch into with me. Everything came tumbling down because a scorned bitch decided to interrupt my life over a man. I felt a hand run up the side of my leg toward my back, then a kiss on the back of my head. I couldn't help but moan. At the same time, I wanted to blame him for everything.

"I'm sorry," he said, lying down in the bed, pulling me into his chest.

"It's not your fault," I answered.

"Tell me about him."

"Who?" I questioned, lifting up only wearing a t-shirt and socks in bed. My hair was all over the place. As soon as I got home and cried my eyes out, my makeup smeared, I removed it in the shower.

"Raymond. Tell me everything about you."

"How much time do you have?" I joked, tracing circles on his chest.

"I have no place to be, you're my client. I'm here to listen."

The statement caused me to pause; I was just a client to him. The way he held me the other night, I felt something other than a client and bodyguard. Was I naive to think after one night of sex, he'd want to try and see if we could date in the real world?

"That's right; I'm just a client," I stated, trying to move out of his arms, and sit up. Dominic shook his head and pulled me in closer, turning our position with him on top. Automatically my legs opened for him.

"I didn't mean it like that, princess. Honestly, I'm confused and not sure what's happening between us. Until Jacinda popped up, I swore off every connection with a woman again besides a few hookups. Before you say anything, what happened between us wasn't a hookup," he responded, running his thumb across my bottom lip.

"How can you say that?"

"Because I didn't meet you at a hotel and never

called you again unless I wanted to see you. That's my normal routine. I don't bring women to my house, nor do I go there. A straight fuck is the only thing they've gotten in the past," he said.

Peering into his eyes, I trusted he was telling the truth.

"Raymond and I dated for about three years. We met at a club one night before things really blew up for me on the internet. At one point, I thought we would get married, over time he changed. It was a mixture of fame and me not wanting to be tied down because I was finally seeing how my life was going in the direction I'd been wanting for so long. Becoming a wife was not my goal. He didn't understand that and started acting out more and more."

"Did he hurt you?" he questioned.

"No, he would do slick little shit like not show up for me when I needed him. Not support me at events. I helped him out and let him stay with me when he lost his job until he could get back on his feet, and a few times, I saw him out with his friends rather than focusing on getting his life together," I said, my mind drifting back to an incident from three years ago.

"Novah, hold my purse for me. I need to run to the restroom," I said, shoving my purse into her lap. Today, I was hosting a club event for this new clothing brand. I do sponsorship ads on

my social media. They invited me to hang out for a few hours with the fans and take pictures.

The music was pumping loud; people were dancing on top of each other. This was the hottest club in town. I wore a custom design created by a local fan. I started posting about her on my page, and she sent me several outfits. Weaving through the crowd, I happened to look up and saw my Raymond, my boyfriend for the past two years, dancing with some woman I'd never met. All of his friends were sitting around, egging them on. He lied and told me he was visiting his parents tonight. Instead of waiting in the long line for the bathroom, I marched up the stairs to his section. They had security around, but everyone knew this party was for me. The security guard removed the rope, and I stomped over to them and slapped the drink out of her hand.

"WTF!" she screamed, jumping up in my face.

"Try it, and I'll have you thrown out," I spat, pointing my finger in her face. Raymond jumped up, gripping my elbow, pushing me away from his date.

I jerked out of his hold and smacked him across the face.

"Damn! Lauren, calm the fuck down," he screamed, pushing us into the corner.

"No! You lied to me and said you'd be with your parents. What the hell do I look like to you? Huh! BooBoo the fool? What's up with you, Raymond?" I snapped, pushing him in the chest to give me space.

"Look, I was with my parents, and then my boys called me to hang out. Not a big deal."

I scoffed, rolling my eyes.

"How are you hanging out with no job? You've laid up in my bed for the past few months not working, complaining about me, and then lying to go hang with your bum friends," I stated, motioning toward his friends.

"You've changed, and I'm not with all this in your fake bullshit. You are constantly gone, posting your ass on every social media platform around. You need to quit this shit, and we can get married. I'm looking for a wife, not an internet model," he demanded.

"Keep looking for that wife then, I'll gladly leave the position open. I'm doing what I love, and you're an ass because you won't grow up and be a grown-up about the situation," I said, walking away and not looking back.

"What happened afterward?" Dominic asked, looking intensely into my eyes.

"I packed his things up and sent them to his parents. I will never apologize for the work I do. I love being creative and meeting people, coming up with products that I like to use and telling my fans that I treat like family about them," I answered, leaning up to kiss his lips. He pulled back in surprise.

"What's wrong?" I questioned.

"I don't want you doing something you'll regret later. Maybe we shouldn't overcomplicate things until all of this is over."

"You wanted to talk, right?"

"Yeah."

"Then tell me about you and your family. You already met my parents and brother. Plus, that bitch Jacinda. I need every detail," I said, gliding a hand between us and reaching under his shirt. He smirked, bending down, kissing me again, and rolling over on his back. I slid my leg over his thigh, rubbing up and down his chest as he talked.

CHAPTER SEVENTEEN

Dominic

Dealing with the past can only help to heal the future, it's what my father used to tell me all the time when I was growing up and when I went into the navy. The things I saw over in Iraq still fucked me up from time to time. Now here I was, possibly opening myself up to someone that could hold all my secrets and cause me even more hurt or happiness if we fell out.

"My dad's retired military and a police officer. My mother is a stay-at-home woman. I have an older brother, Desmond, who's a cop, married with two kids. A younger sister around your age. She's obsessed with you. I haven't told her I was hired to be your security. She'll probably kill me when I do."

"Is Desmond as sexy and tall as you?" she questioned, running her hand up to my chin.

"Don't be asking about my brother, woman," I

teased, smacking her ass. She laughed and rubbed the sting away.

"You didn't answer the question, so he must be sexier than you," she taunted, unbuckling my belt. I grasped her chin, forcing her to look into my eyes.

"He gets his looks from our parents the same as me. Anyway, I've never been married, dated on and off for a year once I came back home, and Jacinda was my longest relationship."

"Was this at *Maven* magazine?" she inquired.

"We met when she was doing a story on Iraq with a newspaper, and she interviewed Mark and me. Things hit off, and we went out on a few dates and became a couple right after. Somehow, she lost her job at the newspaper and went toward the gossip rag magazine. I was prepared to get married and make her my wife. Instead, Jacinda wanted fame, fortune, and title only."

"What do you mean?"

"My family's name is highly respected in the community and Virginia. I don't flaunt where I come from, and she wanted to use that to her advantage and expected to become this socialite that could get anything without working for it. Eventually, she cheated, got pregnant, and pretended it was my kid until I caught on and confronted her."

"Are you serious?!" Lauren covered her mouth in surprise.

I nodded in answer.

"Even after I caught her and she said it was over, she continued to see the guy."

"Wow! I know we have scandalous women in the world, but damn. So, she's doing all this to get you back and make me look bad?" Lauren concluded.

"I don't do this, and it's that simple. She's out for revenge, no doubt. I don't think she wants me back out of love, probably more for convenience, and to say she won."

"She's messing with the wrong woman. I was prepared to sit back and lock myself in my room and cry over how much of a disaster this has been, but I'll figure out a plan to change things around," she said, pushing her hands into the slit of my boxers.

"What are you doing, princess?"

"Putting you to sleep," she teased, removing the comforter off the bed and sitting up, stroking my dick.

"Are you sure about this? I know we are still getting to know each other, Lauren. I do like you, and hell, I tried not to think about you from the first moment we bumped into each other in Virginia. There are many reasons why we wouldn't work as a couple."

"Shut up," she quipped.

"Make me shut up, princess."

Why did I even say that last statement? It was a good thing I was ready for the challenge. I just threw down because her full sweet lips wrapped around my dick and I almost wanted to moan at the pleasure she was giving. I brushed a palm over her back; my stomach retracted at her soft hands caressing my balls. Groans came out in more breathy moans. Her delicate touch was my undoing. I fought between wanting to thrust my dick into her mouth and fucking her senseless for sucking my dick so good.

"Ughhh...princess!" I moaned, gripping the side of the railing and thinking of something else so that I wouldn't come too early. I was weak to her touch.

"Mmmmmm," she moaned out.

She turned to look up at me, popping my dick out of her mouth. Clutching her shirt, I pulled her in closer for a kiss. I covered her lips, tangling our tongues into a rhythmic dance. Straddling my lap, she sank down on top of my dick, biting her lip moaning, pumping up, while I reveled in the ecstasy of being ensconced in her sweet pussy. Removing her shirt, I claimed her breasts in my hands. I pulled her flush against me, feeling each soft curve mold to my body.

"Ohhh!!!!Yessss...Dominic...mmmm."

The pleasure erupted through me, making me growl unexpectedly. I switched, moving her to her back, my breathing rough, my blood surging. I thrust faster. Latching onto her breast, the stare she gave me sent a jolt up my spine.

"I need you, princess," I whispered, and she let out a loud groan. Lauren lifted her leg, wrapping it around my back. Something in my chest twisted, and I roared.

"Oh shit! Baby."

"You make me feel safe, Dominic," she spoke, gripping the back of my neck.

"I know, baby," I answered with an exasperated sound low in my throat.

There was something so sexy in that vulnerable look in her eyes.

Two hours later, she was wearing my shirt, pouring the stir fry rice and orange chicken on our plates, and I wore only my pants. She had me laughing as she mocked me from the first time we met.

"I wasn't that bad. You should have been paying attention." I waved at her phone, which started vibrating. I picked it up and it showed a new message.

"Check it, I trust you," she said. I held it up so she could unlock it, and I tapped on the messages seeing something from a number not saved.

Unknown: I know you're with him.

Me: Who is this?

"You think it's your ex-boyfriend?" I questioned, showing her the message.

"At this point, it could be anyone," Lauren replied.

"Zoe wants you to get on the Raven Cosmetics social pages and make some posts. I think this is the perfect moment to post something to lure them out."

"What should I say?"

"Ask a basic question that you normally do. Emmanuel is already tracing your phone; maybe we can track the number back when you post if someone responds oddly," I said, handing her phone over. I grabbed my phone out of my pocket to tell Emmanuel to start pulling a trace on her calls.

"Okay, I just posted from the account."

She handed the phone over to me, and I saw her post- Lauren A + Raven Cosmetics. The post was liked a hundred thousand times and retweeted five hundred thousand times with comments pouring in and looking over at her phone, I saw that a new message had popped up.

Unknown: Will finally meet at the launch party!

Me: Stop playing on my phone, Raymond.

"They're getting bolder," I said.

Her phone dinged and Zoe's name came across the screen.

"Hey, Zoe," Lauren said as she answered.

Lauren placed the call on speaker, taking a bite of her food. She came around and sat next to me. I kissed the side of her cheek.

"Hello, Queen, how are you feeling?" Zoe questioned over the phone.

"I'm good here, hanging with Dominic." I winked, she leaned over, kissing my lips.

"Hey, Zoe."

"Glad she's in good hands. I saw your post, and your numbers are running through the roof. Keep it up, and don't let what happened earlier get you down. I've been there with being betrayed by an ex. I'm sending the details of the party to you right now. I have a few hashtags you should use and if you're comfortable with a quick video, I think that would be a good idea as well," Zoe commented.

"Sounds good."

"Danielle was able to get them taken down," Zoe stated.

"Thanks, I never knew he recorded us. I was shocked he'd stoop that low and sell me out like that," Lauren replied.

"You remember when it happened?" I questioned, grabbing a piece of paper to take notes. She nodded and continued talking.

"It was for his birthday. I didn't know he was recording, but I remember he was really pushing for me to take naked photos for his birthday, and I said I only do swimsuit photos."

"Sounds like a prick, reminds me of my ex, Timothy," Zoe said.

We laughed at her response.

"Hey, Zoe, send me the information about the

party. I'll have Emmanuel do a sweep first. Make sure Danielle knows," I requested.

"All right, D. Be safe and take care of her," Zoe replied.

"Always," I answered.

Lauren put the plate down and stood between my legs. I wrapped my arms around her waist.

"Sure you want to take on a spoiled, social media celebrity influence? The public is demanding of my every move," Lauren asked.

"As long as you respect my privacy and work, I can make this work."

"What are you doing tomorrow?" Lauren asked.

"I have to do some interviewing and do a sweep of the venue before the party."

Lauren pecked my lips, then asked, "Afterwards?"

"Dinner at my folks' house."

"Invite them to the party. I'd like to meet them," Lauren said.

"Baby, my parents aren't the partying type."

"It would be fun; my folks are coming back down from New York."

"Let me think about it, okay?"

She agreed, moving out of my arms and taking our plates to the sink.

"Where's Novah? I didn't hear her at all last night," I stated, picking up our glasses, following behind.

"I don't know. She probably met someone."

"Does she do that often?"

"Okay, Mr. Bodyguard, calm down. Let Novah get her groove back. We just finished up multiple rounds this morning. I'm still sore; I think she's fine."

"I can't turn it off, babe. Besides, some shit is going on with you having a stalker, can't take any chances."

"Appreciate you for being on top of things, but Novah-"

The door opened, and Novah walked through with Emmanuel behind her.

CHAPTER EIGHTEEN

Lauren

She was wearing the same outfit she wore yesterday. On top of that, she was smiling really hard, carrying a bag of food.

"Where have you been?" I asked, walking toward her.

"Sorry, but I couldn't take the crying and moaning from you two most of the night and got up to head for breakfast and hang out with Emmanuel," Novah stated.

I glared at her, while Emmanuel threw his hands up signifying that he wasn't in on the joke.

"That's my cue to get going," Emmanuel said, turning around, heading back out. Dominic chuckled, and I slapped him on the arm.

"That's not funny."

Tugging me close, I fell into his arms, pouting with my lip poked out.

"Spoiled baby," Dominic commented, kissing my lips.

"You two haven't had enough of each other?" Novah said, putting her food in the fridge.

"She's right. I need to get over to Raven and check over the tapes. Yesterday was just the beginning, and somebody's playing with us, and I don't like it," Dominic told me.

"Was Raymond involved?" Novah asked.

"We don't know for sure," I answered, following Dominic to my bedroom. He opened the door, grabbing his shoes, keys, and wallet off my bed. After we had sex earlier this morning, I changed the sheets and showered, putting his shirt on. Sleeping in his arms gave me peace and comfort beyond what I ever had with Raymond.

Dominic slid his phone in his pocket, and I tried removing his shirt, but he stopped me.

"Keep it; I like knowing I have something over here. Remember, don't leave unless Emmanuel is driving you. If he can't make it, come get me," Dominic commanded, kissing my forehead.

"Okay," I said.

Walking out of my bedroom, I sat down on my couch next to Novah.

"Remove the frown, girl, that man will be back.

Based on what I heard last night, he's sprung, sweetie," Novah joked.

"We were that loud?"

She busted out laughing, nodding her head.

"I'm so embarrassed. He's the best I've ever had, and he's so sweet and tender, making sure I'm pleased. That mouth, girl!"

"You look happy; well, separate from the bullshit with that article."

"Jacinda bitch can kiss my ass. She's not going to win."

"That's what I like to hear. What are you wearing to the party?"

"I have no idea. My parents will fly back in two days. I need to make sure we pull a stylist for them," I remarked before making a mental note to do just that.

"I know they're proud of you, even if you don't see it all the time."

"How are things with the accounting business?" I asked.

She smiled. "Things are coming together. I found a few office spaces for rent. I appreciate you lending me the money to rent the space. I'm planning on interviewing for an assistant, have you looked into hiring someone full-time as an assistant?"

"It's on my list."

I knew I wouldn't have her around me all the time helping me navigate these waters, but it was nice to have my best friend become her own boss like me.

"Come on, let's do a quick video I can post on my page. I already have hits on my post. Then we can call up my stylist to bring a few pieces over so we can look them over."

Grabbing my phone, I checked over my face, pleased I didn't look too tired and decided to do a natural video to upload.

"Hey fam, this is your girl, Lauren. I know a lot has gone on over the past day or two. But I'm here to let you know that Lauren and the Raven Cosmetics launch party is coming soon. Stay tuned. Smoochies!" I announced, smiling with Novah next to me, and I saved it to upload from my computer.

Closing my phone, I stood up, walking to my bedroom. Novah held a notepad and pen to take notes.

"What color are you wearing?" I asked Novah.

"Whatever you want me to wear. It's your night, L. Please don't stress."

"We should all coordinate the colors; the party theme is old Hollywood, a lot of white, red, and gold colors. Make sure we tell the stylist to bring enough pieces we can choose from, and I'll need a second outfit just in case we have an after party."

"Okay."

"What's up with you and Emmanuel?" I questioned.

She walked over and sat down on my bed.

"You can't say anything, Lauren. I know your big mouth."

"Tell me. I'll keep it a secret."

"Fine, I have a small crush on him. But don't get all crazy on me and try to hook us up."

"I can count on my hand how many guys you've dated. He seems sweet from the moments we've been around each other. What does it say about you?"

"Not much, he's a workaholic, and we've only talked a few times. So, don't go planning a wedding," Novah joked.

"Well, Dominic and I are going to try dating. If you can call it dating, with everything going on."

"He's good for you. You need someone calm when you're tense and need to be brought back down to earth."

"I'm not that bad, girl. He's worried about the age difference," I said, pinching her arm.

"I thought he was killing you the way you two were screaming last night."

"Novah, ahhh!! Shut up," I screamed, bursting out in laughter, covering my eyes in embarrassment.

"A good man will do that to you," she commented.

"Let me call April so she can come with some outfits for the party. You are too much," I said, texting on my phone.

"We should go to the mall. I need a few things,"

Novah said. I nodded as my phone rang, and her voicemail came on. I decided to leave a message instead.

"*Hey, April, call me back; the party is still on, and I need your help. Bye*!" Grabbing my keys and putting on some pants and shoes, we left to find Emmanuel sitting in his car.

"Ladies, how can I assist you today?" Emmanuel asked, leaning out of the driver's seat.

"Shopping, please," I begged, poking out my lips and making prayer hands.

"Let Dominic know, and we can go," Emmanuel responded.

I sent Dominic a text once I was in the car and buckled.

Me: Heading to the mall with Emmanuel.

Dominic: See you later for dinner.

Me: You cooking?

Dominic: Only if I can eat it off you.

I cackled to myself.

Me: You're nasty.

Dominic: Just for you, princess.

“Shit!” Emmanuel muttered lowly.

“What’s wrong?”

“Damn paparazzi. Just don’t pay attention to them, and you’ll be fine,” Emmanuel said.

“I can’t believe you have to deal with that, Lauren. I’ll stick to my little accounting job,” Novah commented.

Emmanuel arrived at the mall a few minutes later. He pulled up in front of the main entrance and let us out.

“Let me park; you guys stay right here,” Emmanuel stated, parking near the front entrance. We stepped out, and I put my shades on and pulled my ponytail out to cover my face. A few seconds later, Emmanuel walked up and held the door open for us; we stepped inside.

“We should try the shoe store first; I need some things for the house and a few personal items,” Novah said, locking her arm with mine.

“I hope you ladies aren’t planning on being here all day,” Emmanuel retorted.

“Emmanuel, I have no credit limit, and I’m a celebrity if you haven’t noticed. I get things for free, so plan on being here for a while, buddy,” I said, moving my shades down, winking my left eye.

“Pray for me now,” Emmanuel mumbled under his breath.

"Lauren! OMG! It's Lauren; can we have an autograph?" a group of women shouted, walking up to us.

"Yes sure, you have a pen?" I asked.

"I'm a huge fan and can't wait to see the launch of the makeup. Will it stream on your channel?" the leader of the group asked.

"We are, and Raven Cosmetics is having a contest afterward, so you have to stay tuned," I replied. They were taking pictures after I autographed all three of their photos.

"So excited, I loved the photoshoot you did on the beach," she told me.

"Time for us to go. Dominic texted me to get you back home," Emmanuel cut in and said. I nodded and waved goodbye to the girls.

Three hours later, we arrived back home with multiple bags from six different stores. I flopped down on the couch, kicking off my shoes.

"Go take a nap, now, because tomorrow you have a lot going on with trying on dresses and your family arriving," Novah said.

"You're right, I need to get my beauty rest. Dominic wants me to have dinner with his family, and I invited them to the party," I said, standing up and yawning, walking off toward my bedroom, shutting the door, and falling on the bed to go to sleep.

CHAPTER NINETEEN

Lauren

The next day, I finally finished trying on different outfits for the party tomorrow. April came over with at least twenty different gowns for us to choose from. My parents and brother were hanging with Novah at the beach. I had a prior commitment for dinner with Dominic and his family tonight. Closing my car door, I saw the front door open and a little girl with Dominic, behind him, grinning, was standing there. The place was nice, simple, and cozy, a brick one level home with a two-car garage.

"Lauren you're pretty," the little girl said. I bent down to her level and pinched her nose. She giggled and ran back into the house. Dominic held his hand out to help me inside. I wore my favorite heels and a long wrap dress. Meeting his parents was a new level for us, and I didn't want to come off as some big time diva.

"Thank you for coming," Dominic told me as he bent down and buried his face in my neck. I giggled at him grabbing my ass.

"Stop, your parents are right around the corner. You're not getting me in trouble."

He pulled back, licking his lips.

"When this is over, I'm peeling you out of this dress," he said, placing his hand on top of mine, walking me further inside.

"I'll hold you to that."

Loud laughter and kids screaming made me wish I was a kid again when things were simpler. Dominic cleared his throat.

"Family, I'd like you to meet someone," Dominic started to say when a woman started to scream and jump up and down. I was a bit shocked, but I was kind of used to getting recognized when I was out.

"OMG! It's really you. I didn't believe him when he first told me. You never post pictures of the people you're dating. Dominic, you're dating Lauren Armstrong. Wait until I tell my friends," she said.

"Devan, right?" I replied and she nodded. I reached out for a hug and she started screaming again.

"Devan, calm down, she's a regular person like the rest of us," Dominic said, wrapping his arm around my shoulder, pulling me in closer. Devan raised an eyebrow at him.

"Shut up, Dominic. This the most important thing you've ever done for me," she joked, and Dominic jerked back in surprise. She tried to reach over and hug him and he pushed her away. I chuckled, hugging him and kissing his lips to make him feel better.

"I'm the most important thing you've ever given her," I whispered against his lips.

"Don't mind Devan, she can be a little shallow."

"I recall you saying the same thing about me, Mr. Combs," I teased.

"You still are, but I like that shit."

We both laughed at his statement. A man that I assumed was his brother walked over with another gentleman.

"Hey, Lauren, you have to forgive our sister. She was dropped on her head when she was young. Desmond, the older brother."

"Nice to meet you, Desmond," I replied.

"Lauren Armstrong, baby, it's a pleasure to meet you. I'm Elias, the cousin and best friend. Do you have any sisters, cousins, or aunties?" Elias asked and Dominic removed my hand out of his cousin's and pushed me behind him. I laughed so hard; Elias had no shame.

"Elias, stop making a fool of yourself. Let that girl

come in here and relax for a change without you hounding her," another woman's voice stated.

"Baby, this is my mom and dad. Sonya and Drake Combs." Dominic introduced us.

I shook their hands and she motioned for me to take a seat. Dominic held out my chair and I sat next to him with his brother and cousin on the opposite side with the kids next to them.

"Lauren, my son tells me you're a model?" Sonya questioned, passing the salad dressing around the table.

"I'm a social media model and influencer. I recently became an ambassador to a makeup company and have the chance to create my own line. Actually, I'd love for your entire family to come to the launch party," I replied.

"Devan, let's get something straight in front of everyone. Lauren is my girlfriend. She's not here to play dress up with you. Find your little friends and leave my girl alone," Dominic fussed.

I slapped him on the shoulder for being rude.

"I can hang with your sister. She's not doing anything wrong. Be nice."

"Thanks, Lauren. He's always trying to stop my shine," Devan told me.

I nodded. "No worries, we have to stick together. I have a younger brother so I understand how annoying they can be."

Dominic leaned over and whispered in my ear, "Don't get your ass on punishment." Then he kissed the side of my face.

"I like her Dominic; she doesn't take shit from you. How old are you, young lady?" Sonya asked.

"Twenty-five, Ma'am."

"That's young, are you ready for a relationship with the type of man Dominic is and the lifestyle he leads?" his mother questioned.

"We already covered that, Mom. She was the one that pursued me," Dominic said, taking a bite of his salad while I pinched his leg underneath the table.

"Ouch!" he shouted. Everyone looked over at him and I pretended to innocently drink my water.

"How was the walk through of the hotel?" I asked him.

"It was good. The ballroom of the Ocean View Hotel is letting us have a couple of suites on top of the party room. So, you can get changed and dolled up. Zoe has the red carpet confirmed and Emmanuel will be there for that while I take care of the inside," Dominic explained.

"You're not going to walk with me?" I asked, poking my lip out in a pout. He leaned over and kissed my lips and everyone whistled and hollered in joy.

"Sorry, baby, not this time. I need to make sure you're safe on all sides."

As the night went on, we laughed, talked, and

drank until it was time for us to leave. An hour later, Dominic had me bent over in the shower fucking me senseless as the water dripped down our bodies.

"Shit! Lauren.... Damn, I can't stop," he groaned, gripping my hips as his thrusts sped up.

"I know, keep going. Fuck!" He pulled me up, placing my hands on the wall as he stroked the upper mound of my breast. My thighs spread wider as his other thumb circled my clit. I came apart at the sound of our flesh smacking. I felt the first hint of my orgasm coiling at my stomach, whimpering as he drove deeper.

"Ahhhh! Lauren!" he shouted, as he came inside of me. We stood out of breath, as his dick went limp and slid out as the water started to get cold.

"OMG! Yessss...Mmmmmm."

"I need another shower after that," he joked.

"That's true and I'll let you go alone first," I turned to say, and he lifted my chin, kissing me deeply. I pulled back.

"That's what got us here in the first place. Finish showering, I'm ready for bed," I remarked, stepping out and grabbing a towel before I headed to Novah's room to shower and change.

CHAPTER TWENTY

Lauren

Two days later, it was the day of the party. I couldn't relax from all of the nervousness about making sure everything went off without a hitch. My parents were dressed and at the hotel so Novah and I were getting ready to head out in the car to meet up with Danielle and Zoe after they called me earlier to check my progress. I had my hair slicked in a mermaid ponytail with the new Raven Spicy Red lipstick and body glow. April picked out a short spaghetti-strapped red dress and gold gladiator heels, with matching gold clutch. A car stopped in front of the Ocean View Hotel as a long line of people were posing on the carpet. The photographers were standing getting shots and interviewing Danielle and Zoe. Our door opened and Emmanuel held his hand out for me to take.

"Thanks."

"Are you ready for this?" Emmanuel asked.

"Only time will tell. Is Dominic here?" I inquired.

Novah stepped out behind me and Emmanuel smiled at her. I shook my head at those two. Zoe spotted me and waved me over toward the interviewer.

"The lady of the hour is here," Zoe said, hugging me.

"You look gorgeous, Zoe," I replied.

"Thank you. I was surprised that Dominic let you out looking like this," Zoe said, pointing to my outfit.

"He left before I got ready today."

"Lauren, how are you feeling about the launch of the line?" the reporter asked, holding the microphone out to me.

"I feel great, this is an amazing opportunity for me. My family and friends are here to support me." I gestured to Novah and my family taking pictures and walking inside. Danielle came over and I hugged her.

"Let's get some photos together," Danielle suggested.

I nodded stepping back on the red carpet on the step, posing next to Danielle. They had servers standing outside with sample lipsticks for anyone that walked up to try on along with the body glow.

"Over here, Lauren, to the left, the side," the photographers yelled.

We stood out there for fifteen minutes answering questions and talking about the line. Zoe shut it down when they started talking about the sex tape and article.

"That's enough, guys, if you have any more questions, you can email my office," Zoe stated, walking next to us.

"This is so overwhelming," I said.

"I expected that to happen, don't let them get to you. Tonight's all about a new beginning," Zoe informed me.

"I agree with Zoe, you look stunning and already the online orders are coming in and we sold a million lipsticks in twenty minutes. Obviously, what we're doing is working," Danielle stated.

Looking around, the place was beautifully decorated. "I love the hanging lights, Zoe," I commented. There were low hanging lights and a big poster of the beach shoot in the background. I felt my phone vibrate, so I removed it out of my clutch and saw a message from Dominic.

Dominic: Meet me upstairs.

Me: Aren't you supposed to be working?

Dominic: Securing you in every way is my job.

I smirked. Looking around the room, I figured I could sneak out for a few minutes.

Me: Okay, what suite number?

Dominic: 203, princess.

Me: Coming now.

"I'll be right back. I need to slip to the ladies' room."

"Take Emmanuel with you."

"I'll be fine, too many people around for anything to happen to me."

"All right, I will wait to do the intro until you come back," Danielle called out.

Slipping off around the corner, I stepped on the elevator and headed up to the suite that Dominic reserved for us. A few seconds later, the doors opened, and I stepped off walking down the hall and knocked on the door. I checked the handle and saw it was already open. He must have gotten it ready for me knowing I was coming up. Opening the door, I walked inside and saw candles lit all around. I covered my face in shock.

"Dominic, this is beautiful. Where are you?" I remarked, shutting the door.

"Not here," I heard a woman's voice announce, and I turned to see Carol pointing a gun at me. Her face held a hard glare.

"Carol! Where's Dominic?" I questioned, nervously stepping toward the door.

"Stop moving!" she shouted.

I jumped, stopping in my tracks. "Sorry, okay. What are you doing?"

"I'm claiming what's mine. I'm tired of being dismissed and pushed to the side. You're not worthy of being the face and taking all of my ideas and becoming the star. I'm done fighting for my position to be the CEO of Raven."

"I'm not the enemy, Carol, put the gun down and let's talk about this." I tried to step back slowly toward the door.

"Stop talking! I knew if I could get Jacinda to pick up a story about you and cause a little interruption in the media, they would drop you and let me step in like I wanted in the first place. She's too high up Dominic's ass to see the bigger picture. Even those text messages they traced went back to her phone. I had everything planned out to get you to quit on your own and you didn't. So now I have no choice but to end you," Carol stated.

"You were the one that sent the first message talking about being my biggest fan?" I asked, remembering how the first one started right before I signed my contract.

"I didn't expect for them to bring in a security

team and Josslyn's dumb ass kept emailing me about the formulas changing on her shifts."

"You purposely shipped out a bad product to see the company fall."

"Raven Cosmetics would be nothing without me!" she screamed.

CHAPTER TWENTY-ONE

Dominic

Signing off on the last round of guests inside the party, I headed over to check in with Danielle and Zoe in the ballroom. My family was laughing and dancing with Novah and Emmanuel, and Lauren's parents near the stage. I looked around and didn't see Lauren with them and that wasn't like her to not be in the center stage. Tapping Danielle on the shoulder, she turned, giving me a one arm hug.

"How is everything looking?" she asked.

"Everything is good, and we haven't had any issues all night. Where's Lauren?"

"She said she was going to the bathroom, but that was fifteen minutes ago. You think something's wrong?" Her brow creased in worry.

"Raven Cosmetics went all out for the party tonight, I see," Jacinda spoke, grabbing a glass of champagne off the tray the waitress held. I took it out of her hand and told her she didn't need it.

"Who invited you?" Zoe asked.

"I'm a part of the media, Zoe. *Maven* magazine is still a repetitive media outlet, don't be mad because we exposed your clients," Jacinda spat.

Zoe glared at her, pressing her lips together in anger.

"Ladies, let's not do this tonight," I said, grasping Jacinda's arm and pointing to security.

"Let me go. I have the right to be here like anyone else!" Jacinda spat.

"We sent private invitations to selected magazines and you were not one of them. I suggest you get out of here before things get ugly," Zoe stated. Mark walked up to all of the back and forth conversation. I was getting annoyed and frustrated because Lauren wasn't here.

"Shooter, do we have a problem?" he questioned.

"No, just your hired employees are trying to intimidate me," Jacinda replied, crossing her arms.

"I need to look for Lauren, we have a presentation in five minutes," Danielle called out and I nodded, following behind her.

"Too late," Jacinda chuckled hauntingly, causing me to stop walking.

"What does that mean?" I questioned.

"I mean your little girlfriend is no longer a part of

Raven Cosmetics or the living if my calculations are correct. She was disposed of, a few minutes ago," Jacinda stated, checking her watch.

"What did you do?" I yelled, gripping her neck. She tried to push me off of her as Mark and Emmanuel tried to talk me down.

"Shooter, not here. We'll find her, let her go. Come on, let her go," Mark demanded.

I squeezed a little bit harder and dropped her on the floor. The music stopped, everyone glanced over at what was happening.

"We have to find her," I muttered before running off toward the bathroom.

When I busted inside, Danielle looked under the stalls while I checked the men's room.

"She couldn't have gone far, maybe the suites upstairs!" Danielle stated.

She ran toward the elevator punching the button, but I wasn't waiting for people to get on and off. I marched over to the stairs checking my phone to see what rooms we had secured for the night. Pushing the door of the emergency exit open, I ran out on to the second floor and tried my key for door one and it didn't work. I tried the second door, still nothing, and then I heard a loud scream right as the elevator chimed.

"No!"

Kicking the door of room 203, I saw Lauren and

Carol fighting over a gun when all of sudden a loud bang went off and they both fell down.

"OMG! Call the police," Danielle screamed.

Mark helped me to pull them apart before he kicked the gun away and checked Carol's pulse.

"It's fading, we need an ambulance. Zoe, go downstairs and shut the party down. Give them any excuse, say Lauren got sick or something," Mark commanded.

I turned Lauren over. Her dress was covered in blood and her eyes were closed. I tried to feel for a pulse, and it was weak.

"Baby, talk to me. I'm here, not going anywhere," I said as the EMTs rushed inside. They tried to take Lauren out of my hands and I refused.

"Shooter, they need to work on her, man. I know this is tough but let them do their job. She's safe now," Mark said, with his hand on my shoulder.

"She's not safe because of me," I whispered as I fought back tears.

"What's her name?" one of the EMTs asked.

"Lauren," I heard Danielle say.

This was happening all over again. I was losing someone that I cared about.

"She's crashing, we need to get to the hospital now!" one of the EMTs yelled and they lifted her on the gurney and left the room.

"Are you riding to the hospital with her?" Danielle questioned, rubbing my back.

I shook my head no, looking down at my hands covered in blood from her dress.

"Don't shut down on us now, Shooter. Lauren needs you, man," Mark said, following me out of the hotel room.

Fifteen minutes later, we arrived at the hospital and I still hadn't changed my clothes. Danielle, Mark, Emmanuel, and our families filled the waiting room, wondering when the doctor was going to come back and give an update on her status. I heard when they loaded her up in the ambulance, she crashed.

Mark walked up and passed me a cup of coffee. "Get out of your head, this isn't your fault."

"You know us navy men never take a mission without seeing it through. The second we lose someone, that's a failure," I remarked.

"Love will do that to you."

"Do what?" I questioned.

"Have you guessed every little thing? This would have happened with or without you two being together. I had some men from Cole Security do a sweep of Carol's place and found a lot of shit that she's been doing for the past few years," Mark advised.

"She's been planning this for a while. Emmanuel had our best guys on tracing that number and it led back to Jacinda. When we talked with her, she confessed that Carol approached her about working together, but it was only to scare Lauren and try to get me back. Things took a turn when she saw we hadn't stopped with the launch of the brand."

"Her office was filled with photos of Lauren and different ideas on how to get rid of her by sabotaging the lipstick line. She was even thinking of poisoning the next batch they made. Josslyn was close to finding out about what was going on, because she kept seeing strange discrepancies and mentioned them to Carol and nothing got fixed."

"Probably rigged the camera we installed, because we never saw anything off besides her walking in and out of the camera view," I mumbled, thinking about the same scene playing over and over again.

"What? You remembered something?" Mark asked.

Nodding and walking off, he followed behind.

"Dominic, where are you going? Lauren's going to be looking for you," Devan said.

"Not now, Devan. I'll be back."

I jogged out of the hospital with Mark behind me, getting into my car. We drove off toward my office. Running the red lights, a normal forty-minute drive turned into fifteen minutes and we hopped out.

"What do you think?"

"The tapes, she had to have known about the extra hidden one or manipulated someone to help." I opened my office door and picked up the remote and hit play on the recordings for Raven Cosmetics.

"Tell me what I'm looking at," Mark commented.

"Right there. The time stamp. Remember that number 00021," I called out. Fast forwarding to another date, it was the same thing. Her walking by in the same direction, same movements with her pushing her hair back behind her ear.

"I don't see anything," Mark said.

"That's it."

"What is?"

"She cloned the tapes and manipulated them to have the same sequence so we wouldn't think anything was off because she wore the same outfits, most of the time. The problem is that she wasn't expecting me to catch on that this day, she had a Raven Cosmetics lipstick on, and the other days, she didn't. So, she must have forgotten, and I never paid attention to the little detail because I was distracted," I confessed.

"I know what you're thinking and you're going to regret it. Give yourself some time before you completely throw everything away," he said, pouring a glass of scotch and passing it over to me.

"Tell me why my head and heart are not on the same wavelength, because I fucked up again this time."

"What happened with Jackson is not your fault or mine, all of us couldn't predict he'd get hurt back then. Time heals all wounds and you can't burden yourself with the past."

"I can't look at her and not feel guilty. Fuck! I should have protected her," I shouted, sweeping everything off my desk. I knew they trusted me and because of our friendship in the past and knowing Danielle needed someone that was an expert in reading people and the signs, I completely missed Carol being the stalker because I was too wrapped in my feelings.

My phone rang and I saw it was Emmanuel.

"What's the news?" I asked, taking the sip of the scotch.

"She's awake and she's asking for you," Emmanuel said.

"Thanks, Emmanuel, protect her for me," I replied, hanging up the phone.

"You do this, Shooter, you'll regret it, brother."

I turned my phone off from everybody, sliding it in my pocket.

"I need some time to think. Keep an eye on them for me," I stated, leaving the glass on the desk and walking out of my office.

I hopped in my car and drove home to lock away the events from the past few hours. I was even considering possibly flying out of the country for a few days to get away from everything and everyone. Pulling into my driveway, I shut the car off, staring at the car garage.

"Fuck! *Fuck!*" I shouted, beating my palm against the steering wheel.

Stepping out and heading inside, I turned the alarm off and on, locked the door and stripped out of my clothes before throwing them in the trash. Turning on my voicemail, I heard a call from my mom.

"Son, I know you're hurting, but that's the way to fix things. Lauren needs you and you need her just as much. The second she woke up, she asked for you. Don't let your fear cloud your judgement," Mom said. Grabbing the bottle of scotch off my counter, I walked upstairs to the shower. Seeing Lauren covered in blood while dying in my arms was a sign that I got too complacent and sidetracked. Love would only destroy me in the end. Working was the only thing that I knew would never cause pain like what I saw earlier today.

CHAPTER TWENTY-TWO

Lauren

Three months later and I still hadn't heard from him. I was in Paris for the launch of Raven Cosmetics with Danielle, Zoe, Novah, and Emmanuel. He was there as my personal security guard from Cole Security that Mark requested. From what they told me, Dominic was still working cases, only he handed everything over to Emmanuel that had to do with Raven's accounts. They didn't think I was ready to get back to work, along with the doctor, but I was healing and doing my physical therapy. Most of the events we had were scheduled out in a bi-weekly setting so I could rest up. Today was a small gathering of buyers for local stores looking at the products and interviewing me for the local newspapers. I heard Carol was in jail and the rest of the lab personnel were replaced. Danielle didn't take any chances on someone else leaking or tampering with the products. I had already finished my breakfast for the day, so I was getting ready. I stepped out of the shower and was drying my hair with a towel when I heard knocking on the door and Novah asking to come inside.

"Are you decent, L?"

"Yep, is Emmanuel here?"

She came inside with a bouquet of flowers and placed it on top of the counter.

"Who sent the flowers?"

"Danielle and Zoe sent them to cheer you up," Novah said. I bent over and smelled the roses, smiling at the cute greeting card that said *Queens rise above.* I chuckled. Since I've worked with them over the past few months, we've become closer and created a bond, a really strong friendship.

"Tell them I said thank you. Are they downstairs?" I asked.

Novah nodded, jumping up on top of the counter, picking over my hair products as I picked up the hair dryer and comb.

"Yes, and Emmanuel is waiting in the living room when you're ready to go."

"Thanks, now tell me. How bored are you in Paris? I can see it all over your face," I mentioned, because mostly I've been working and have had less time to hang out with her than I normally would like and she's stuck either coming along with me or eating out at some restaurant and shopping alone.

"Not too bad, but I'm fine. You're more important and making sure the star is ready for her close ups," Novah stated.

I chuckled before replying, "No star over here. After the shooting craziness, I've become even more popular and that tells how crazy our society is that they'd pay more attention to a disaster than the positivity in my life."

"He still hasn't called?" she inquired.

"I think it's best we both move on; we wouldn't have gotten far in a relationship. Not only the age difference, but the little we had in common was outlawed by outside interference. You remember what I went through with Raymond."

"Please don't compare Dominic to Raymond," Novah chastised.

"Why not, it's the same when you think about it. Honestly, the moment things get hard, men run away. Let me change and I'll meet you out there, drop the subject please."

Novah held her hands up in surrender and stood up leaving out of the bathroom as I got dressed.

Forty minutes later, I was at Zoe and Danielle's table discussing business.

“Tell the truth, how tired are you?” Danielle asked me.

The restaurant was beautiful inside the Novotel Paris Centre. A waitress brought over coffee and tea and I declined, waving my hand, since I already ate in my room.

“Truthfully, I love the hustle and bustle of traveling and meeting new people. Do I get tired sometimes? Of course. But the second I see my work on billboards or doing interviews in magazines, I realize I have the best job in the world, and I can’t really complain,” I replied.

“Are you sleeping better now? Novah told us you had nightmares the first few weeks out of the hospital,” Danielle asked.

“Yeah, I hadn’t dealt with anything that serious before in my life so replaying the shooting over and over again was a lot. The doctor told me about a therapist that deals with trauma situations and I spoke with her a few times, plus working has helped keep my mind off the past.”

“You can’t forget about everything. What about Dominic?” Zoe questioned.

I shrugged, not really knowing how to answer that question.

“I mean, he chose to walk away. Was I upset the moment I opened my eyes and he wasn’t there? Yes. Now I get that I’ll never be what he needs. We’re two different people,” I answered.

"Reminds me of Timothy and I when I tried pushing him away and finally coming to my senses after he convinced me we could work to only turn around and break my heart," Zoe commented, looking out of the window.

"What did you do?"

"The only thing I could. At first, I was upset and tried to get him to see we could work, and nothing would change my love for him. Eventually we went to therapy, then I was pregnant. Now we are married and in love," Zoe replied.

"So, you're saying it was an easy road back together?"

Zoe burst out in laughter. "Oh, honey, no. The road was long and painful. Plus, we're both stubborn and we constantly challenged each other. But I knew he was the man for me and would remind him every time we were around each other," Zoe advised.

"It may not be that easy for me."

"Give it some time, Lauren. I know Dominic and he's just as stubborn. Once we get back home, maybe give him a call and talk things through. Missed chances only happen if you never take that step," Danielle stated.

"Who are we meeting today?"

"You have a photoshoot today and then we can head back home. We sold Lauren+Raven to over fifty distribution stores. Things are looking up," Danielle informed me, holding up her glass of orange juice.

We all stood up clinking glasses and cheering for the success of the launches. Two hours later, I was inside the photo studio with Mariah playing on the radio. My hair and makeup were getting prepared as stylists were pulling items for me to try on. The scar from the shooting was still visible and I didn't get any type of cosmetic surgery yet to cover it up. My plan was to first physically heal before I got more surgery and wasn't able to finish the press tour. I removed the robe and slipped into the long sleeve dress that had my back out. Not wearing heels, I stepped up on the white table and crossed my legs. It was a replica of my office and I had a white robe with my name stitched across, to show me as the creator of the line. Bins of Raven lipstick sat around me.

"Ready, Lauren. You look beautiful," the photographer said. I smiled and nodded, tilting my head, pointing at the makeup.

"Give me one with your lips and eyes closed," he demanded.

"How's this?" I asked, flipping my hair to the side with both eyes and lips closed.

"Fabulous, love, keep going. Naturally beautiful," he responded.

Flipping on the opposite side, I turned and looked over my shoulder with my back showing. Everyone started cheering and clapping, I was doing great. We continued for the next four hours filming until it was time for us to catch a flight back home. I changed and went straight to the private jet that Cole Security provided and fell down in the chair, my glasses firmly in place. After buckling up, I promptly fell asleep.

CHAPTER TWENTY-THREE

Lauren

"Lauren, this is a nice surprise," Mom said, opening the door and letting me inside.

"Hey, Mom."

"I thought you were still in Paris?" she asked.

"We just got back, and I had them drop me off here first before we head to Virginia."

"How long are you here for?"

"Just a day, but I wanted to stop by and see how you guys are doing. Where's Kenny Jr. and Daddy?"

"They went to pick up some groceries for me. You don't look like yourself."

"It's called being exhausted from working nonstop and traveling, old lady."

She popped me on the back of the head, and I laughed.

"I'm not an old lady, little girl. Get your mind right. Tell Momma how you're really feeling."

"Okay, really. Novah is good, business is good, and I actually started back up doing more of my videos. We sold the line to some distributors in Paris."

"Nice, but how are you feeling here?" She pointed to my chest.

"When are you guys going to upgrade this house? I have the money and maybe your wardrobe?" I glanced at her, up and down. She popped me in the shoulder this time and I cackled at her harsh frown.

"The minute you admit you want your little boyfriend back."

"I don't know what you're talking about."

"Admit you miss him and go see him. Nothing wrong with being the person that gives in first. Doesn't mean you're weak or wrong. Only shows that you care and want the happiness that you had in the first place."

"What if he doesn't feel the same way? What if he's moved on to someone less crazy?"

"That's true."

"Ma!"

She laughed, reaching over and giving me a hug.

"I'm kidding, baby. You're grown now, I can't fight your battles for you. Would I prefer you with some church going boy and living a simple life with a 9-5 job? Yes, but you've never been a simple child. So, do what you do best and go get your man," she told me.

"When did Vivien Armstrong become so out there?" I questioned, furrowing my eyebrows.

"I was young once and your father wasn't the man that he is now. We only want to protect you from the bad, baby, and unfortunately that's not possible so I can only give you the tools and let you make the decisions on your own. Be happy and we'll love you no matter what."

I kissed her cheek and jumped up grabbing my purse to head back out to the car to get to Virginia. Life was at a standstill until I made the decision to push forward. The first order of business was confronting Dominic Combs.

The next day, I decided to drop in and find out where we stood. Banging on his door, I waited for someone to come and answer. I got the address from Mark after begging and pleading that I wasn't going to do anything irrational. Shooter was the one that broke my heart. I know one thing about navy men, they protect each other through thick and thin.

"Coming!" I heard someone yell.

I checked my makeup and hair one more time. I wore a simple t-shirt and jeans today with my hair pulled up in a messy bun. Seeing me in regular clothes was a shock to myself, because I'd normally want to be seen at all times in full makeup and glamour. Today, something else was more important.

"What are you doing here, princess?" he asked, standing at the door blocking me from seeing inside. He had someone here. I shouldn't be pissed, but I was, and I was ready to kick his ass and hers. I pushed him back walking inside, not waiting to get an invitation. Removing my shades, I looked around, admiring his home. More a bachelor pad like I thought, black and silver, living connected open space, wide archway leading to the back, possibly his office and stairs across the way and kitchen.

"What are you doing, Lauren?"

"What happened to princess?" I spat, shoving him back, with his presence so close I didn't know if I would fall for his charm all over again and forget why I was here.

He sighed, running a hand down his face.

"I-" I cut him off before he gave me some fucked up excuse.

"You listen. Sit down and wait your turn." I pointed to the couch. His eyes rose in shock, and he bit his bottom lip. Crossing my arms, I stared right back.

"Lauren, I apologize for not being there when you needed me most. I was a fool and I admit that. The second I saw you lying in blood, I completely lost it and couldn't bear to hear the doctor tell me you were dead."

"I'm standing right here, Dominic, and it's three months later and still not a call, text, note, card. *I needed you*!" I screamed, pounding his chest. Gripping my hands, he pulled me in close kissing my forehead, cheek, cupping my face, placing tender kisses on my lips.

"I know that, baby, and I'm sorry. Sometimes, I shut people out and I let it go on too long with you. I never stopped caring about you."

"So, why leave? Huh? I asked for you when I woke up in the hospital."

I pulled away, wiping my face and walking over to the fireplace.

"I told Emmanuel and Mark to watch over you. I always had eyes on you."

"They weren't *you*!" I shouted, throwing the vase of flowers at his head.

"You're right, please forgive me, baby. I'll do anything to make it up to you. I haven't been able to sleep or eat, not seeing your face every day. Hearing you talk about what outfit you're wearing or us arguing about you taking a picture of me," he joked.

I chortled at his statement, he reached out his palm and I placed mine on top, letting him pull me in close.

"How do we get past this?" I questioned.

"With me forgiving myself and asking for your

forgiveness. Then we decide that together is where we want to be."

"What about you coming back on board my security detail?" I asked, wrapping my arms around his chest.

"I can do that." He bent down kissing my lips, gripping my ass.

"Good, because you owe me backrubs, foot massages, and more as payment for fucking up. Normally I would drop a guy in a second that ignores my calls and messages."

Dominic laughed hugging me close.

"How was Paris?" he asked, letting me go and walking toward the kitchen. I followed behind him.

"It was good. I had fun, but mostly worked. Did you cook?"

"Yeah, I wasn't expecting any company. I can split it with you." He grabbed a second plate out of the cabinet.

"I haven't had much of an appetite either."

"Everything all right?"

"Yeah, just dealing with a broken heart because my so-called boyfriend left me."

"You're going to milk this for a while, aren't you?" he asked.

"I wouldn't be Lauren Armstrong if I didn't get something out of this situation that didn't include diamonds," I said, winking at him.

"Princess, don't get cocky."

"You like it when I get cocky, makes your dick hard. When I told you to sit down and shut up, I saw your dick jump. Don't worry, he's on punishment until I say it's time he becomes reacquainted again with pussy."

"So, you haven't dated anyone since we've been apart?" he asked.

"No, I know it's hard for you to imagine, but when I'm all in with a guy, he's all I think about. Dominic, I love you and I don't want to continue this roller coaster ride. Mark told me your address so you can kick his ass for spilling the beans, Shooter," I confessed.

Dominic pulled me into his lap and kissed the side of my face.

"Twilight and Emmanuel can get away with that. As far as me loving your cockiness, princess, it's because you're spoiled, and I like to see your little nose squint up and lips poke out when you're mad. Something about these lips that drive me crazy. How are you doing?"

He lifted my shirt up to see my scar and rub a hand across it, stood me up and dropped down on one knee, kissing the small scar on my side.

"I still do physical therapy; everything is fine though."

"Lauren, I love you."

He stood up caressing my cheek, peering into my eyes and I rose on the tip of my toes, gripping the back of his neck, claiming what's mine. Dominic Combs was the love of my life.

"Where's your bedroom?" I asked, pulling away.

"Are you sure about this? Well enough to be having sex?" Dominic questioned.

"I can do a lot of things, don't worry."

"I thought I was on punishment," he teased, smacking me on my ass.

"Thinking about it long-term only hurts us both. After not having sex for three months and before that, it was for about a year, I couldn't deprive myself of pleasure," I replied, walking up the stairs admiring the photos of his family on the wall.

"So, you're using me?" he stated, hand on his chest in shock.

"Pretty much, old man," I joked, shrugging my shoulders, removing my shirt and kicking off my shoes.

"Princess..." Dominic stalked over to slowly undo his belt buckle.

"Ahhh! I'm sorry." I laughed when he lifted me up and put me over his shoulder and spanked me. I tried rubbing the sting and he kissed both cheeks. Dropping me on the bed I giggled undoing my pants and taking off my panties.

"Have I told you that I love you lately?" Dominic

spoke and the bed dipped as he bent down hovering over my body.

"I haven't heard a word for the past three months."

"Let me make it up to you."

"I love you, Dominic *Shooter* Combs," I said, leaning up, entwining our lips.

Teasing my mouth open, memories of our last night together flooded my mind. Desire shot through me and I was ready to surrender to his command. A low groan left his lips. I loved when he became undone at the touch of my hand. His erection pulsed as I maneuvered his dick at my entrance. He nudged my legs wider with his knee. My pussy wept with need. I guided him inside and we both moaned at the first encounter of our bodies becoming one again.

"Damn, I missed you," he whispered, kissing along my chest, grasping my breasts out of my bra cups. I arched off the bed, receiving every stroke as he slammed into me. Our lovemaking was slow like we normally were. We both knew we were making up for lost time. He swiveled his hips in a circular motion, pulling me tight against him.

"Yesss!"

"Baby!" Dominic cried out.

I wound my arms around his neck, thrusting upwards, nibbling his ear.

"Don't ever leave me again," I told him.

"Never."

CHAPTER TWENTY-FOUR

Lauren

Two months later, things were going well with Dominic, except I was throwing up constantly and I knew that I could possibly be pregnant. *Was I ready to be a mother? Was he ready to be a father?* We were still getting to know each other again and adding a baby in the mix that he probably wouldn't want is something I wasn't ready to deal with. I flushed the toilet, grabbing my toothbrush and wash towel to clean myself up.

His family was meeting us for lunch at Lynnhaven Fish House today and Emmanuel was still waiting on me outside. Dominic was meeting me at the restaurant since he needed to finish up some work. Over the past few weeks, our families had become familiar and his mom checks up on me from time to time. I even have dinner at their place on Sundays with Dominic. I told him we'd fly out to visit my family next time we both have the time off. Novah was waiting on me in the bedroom for the results. When the timer finally went off, I picked up the pregnancy stick and saw the color turned blue with two lines showing in the little window.

"Wow," I mumbled to myself sitting back down on the toilet, covering my face in my hands. I heard a knock on the door.

"Come in," I said.

Novah walked inside and I pointed to the counter. She picked it up and screamed.

"Yes!"

"I don't know about this, Novah. I'm only twenty-five and still have so much I want to do before becoming a mom."

"What are you saying?" Novah questioned.

I sighed, leaning back and crossing my arms.

"I'm scared."

"You have me and Dominic. Plus, his family is here. You have nothing to be afraid of, Lauren. This is a blessing."

"Easy for you to say. Are you sleeping with Emmanuel?"

"If I was, that's my business and no, we are not sleeping together. Too busy trying to get my business up and running."

"Sorry for being snappy. What if it's a boy and he turns out to be like Dominic? OMG, I'd have two hard-headed men in my life making me crazy. He probably won't let me do anything if I'm pregnant," I muttered.

"That is true, he barely lets you do anything now without him being around. It's his subconscious making up for lost time when you weren't together."

"I know. Funny, I can't get rid of him now, when five months ago, I was begging to get him on the phone."

"He loves you, Lauren, and he'll be a great father to your child. So, finish getting dressed and let's go to lunch."

I agreed and reached out for her to help me up.

"Lauren Armstrong is going to be a mother and I'm going to be an auntie."

"Let's wait to see what the doctor says first. I'll make an appointment tomorrow."

"Are you going to tell him today?"

"No, I'll wait until I have the confirmation. Hate to get him excited if it's not true."

"You need me to go with you?"

"No, I'll be fine. We should go so we're not late and I'll let Danielle know afterwards. This might hinder some plans with the next phase for the makeup line."

Finishing the touches to my face, I changed into another wrap dress that Dominic loved to see me in. I prayed I didn't show any signs of being sick and have everyone questioning me. I slid on my flat sandals and shades to follow Novah out to the car with Emmanuel driving. Novah hopped in the front and I shook my head at those two pretending to not have anything going on.

Emmanuel drove off into traffic and I checked my phone to see a new message from Dominic.

Dominic: I'm at the restaurant, baby.

Me: OMW!

"How are you feeling, Lauren?" Emmanuel asked.

"Good."

"Sure? I heard you throwing up earlier," he replied

I shifted in my seat, clearing my throat.

"Just some bad food. All good now."

We arrived ten minutes later, and Emmanuel parked, getting out and opening the door for Novah and I. She smiled and I pushed her to keep walking and stop flirting. Looking around, it wasn't too busy, and I was grateful for that.

"What?"

"Stop flirting with that man unless you're ready to take it there," I responded.

"What makes you think we haven't already?"

"Ohhh, Novah, tell me everything that happened," I whispered slowly.

"I'm not answering those questions," Novah replied.

"I told you about me and Dominic."

"Yeah and I still have nightmares about it," she joked, and I flipped her off.

Emmanuel opened the front entrance for us, and we walked inside. To my surprise, I saw Danielle sitting with Dominic's family.

"Hey, I didn't know you were going to be here," I said, sitting down next to her.

"It was last minute, and I decided to leave work early to hang with my husband once he gets off," Danielle replied.

"That's great, you should take more time out for yourself."

Dominic came around from the head of the table and kissed me on the lips.

"Hey," I said.

"You wore my favorite dress," he replied, running his hand down my arm.

"Behave."

"I can't promise, princess. You look beautiful though."

"Thank you. How was work?"

"Good, we wrapped up everything at Raven's finally, and everything was shipped off without a hitch. Proud of you, and this lunch is to celebrate your accomplishments."

"Thank you, baby," I pulled him in close by his jacket and whispered.

"Lauren, I ordered the makeup and already love it, you have to do some type of review with your line and I want to be in on it," Devan stated.

"We could do a sleepover with all the girls and test everything out."

"That would be fun," Devan said.

"I just got you back, I'm not going to share you with Devan," Dominic told me.

"Stop being so grumpy. You can be away for one night," Devan insisted.

"Nope, I'll be there in the bedroom, while you have your sleepover and she's sleeping next to me," Dominic responded.

"Then, it's not a sleepover if she has to leave," Devan pouted, poking out her tongue and rolling her eyes.

"You two stop! Lauren, you've gained a little weight since I've seen you last time," Sonya said.

"All that food your son has been cooking," I responded, changing the subject off of my appearance.

"Is that the only reason?" she questioned.

"What other reason could it be, Ma?" Dominic said.

"Nothing, son," Sonya replied.

I picked up the glass of water and gulped it down.

The waitress came over and started passing menus around and I took one even though I wasn't hungry.

"You all right? Just ignore my mother. She's always talking about somebody gaining weight," Dominic said.

"It didn't bother me."

"Tonight, I'll rub your feet when we get home," Dominic responded.

"You'll do more than that, mister."

CHAPTER TWENTY-FIVE

Lauren

All of the news stations and social media sites were posting the launch of Raven Cosmetics. We had every type of press discussing each product in detail and the interviews I did in Paris finally aired. I finally got a doctor's appointment two days later and she was taking blood after I finished peeing in a cup. I had Novah drive me today after convincing Emmanuel it was for a girl thing that I didn't want him to drive me today. Dominic knew I was here for my annual checkup, so I technically didn't lie.

"Lauren, I have your results and congrats are in order. You're pregnant."

I sat up off the stirrups and covered my bottom half.

"I'm pregnant with a baby?" I asked.

"You are and I need to get you prenatal vitamins because you're about two and a half months along."

"OMG! The first time we got back together. We didn't use condoms. Damn."

"Do you think the father will have a problem with you being pregnant?" Doctor Carson asked.

"Honestly I don't know what his reaction would be. I'm in shock and not sure."

"You'll be a great mom, don't stress yourself out. Here's some pamphlets and prescriptions and be sure to make an appointment to come back in a month. With you being shot and recovering still, I want to monitor you as high risk."

"Okay." Dr. Carson passed me the pamphlets and information for first time mothers, and I started to get redressed. Walking out in a daze, I saw Novah drop the magazine and walk over to me.

"What did she say?" Novah asked.

"Pre...gnant," I stuttered, handing her the prescription.

"You look a little pale, Lauren. Maybe you should sit down." I shook my head no.

"I'm fine. I just need to think, let's go."

"So, I'm officially Auntie Novah," she said, wrapping her arm around my shoulder.

After leaving the doctor's office, I came home and took a nap, but that didn't last long so I had Emmanuel drive me to Raven Cosmetics to talk with Danielle about my situation. I shut the car door.

"I won't be long, Emmanuel, you can park here or come inside."

"I can wait," Emmanuel replied.

"Okay."

Heading into the building I showed my badge and walked toward the employee entrance and went around the corner toward Danielle's office. I knocked on the door and she waved me inside.

"I was just thinking about you coming in and having a seat."

"You look happy."

"I am and you'll be very happy as well. We hit our target goal of twenty million sales in four hours. Their project will surpass a hundred million by the end of the night."

"Seriously, in four hours!"

"That doesn't even include the online pre-sales we did or the international market. Lauren, I want to do a second collaboration with you if you're interested. I'm prepared to offer you a contract today."

"I don't know what to say."

"Say yes, Zoe is on the phone with our international markets to see about a second tour. This is bigger than we've ever thought it could be."

"I should tell you that I'm pregnant."

"Congrats! So happy for you."

"Thanks, I know this will mess up my chances of doing any more work with the company."

"Lauren, you're pregnant, not dead. We can work around your schedule and when you get closer to the due date, things can be put on hold. What else is on your mind?"

"Wondering if Dominic will be upset?"

"That I can't answer. I know he loves his niece and nephew and you very much."

"Might cause him to be overly protective or even dump me."

"Dominic loves you and wants to be in your life. He told me about your first encounter in the elevator. The look in his eyes when he talked about you was amazing."

"You're friends with him, tell the truth. After Jacinda's situation, did he ever fall in love with another woman?"

"No, and never compare your present to the past, learn from the mistakes and move forward. Dominic made it clear that he's all in with you now, and I kind of gave him a little warning to not break your heart again or he'd have to deal with me, Zoe, and the other girls."

"Okay, I'll sign. This time, I'll start to have more of a work life balance. Trying to live up to the world of the social media status and celebrity lifestyle is too exhausting. I like my peace and calm with my friends and family. It took me a while to understand."

"That's called maturity," she said, standing up, walking to her desk and picking up what I assumed was a contract for me.

"How long would this one be for?" I asked.

"Take it home and discuss it with Dominic, you have to take his input into consideration now. Plus, about that little cupcake that's baking in your tummy. I put ten years with you having your exclusive makeup line, with over twenty products and another collaboration for the holidays for first rights."

"Danielle, I don't know what to say."

"Say you will think about it and let me know tomorrow."

"Sure. I'll have an answer tomorrow."

"Perfect."

CHAPTER TWENTY-SIX

Dominic

"What's on your mind?" I inquired. We sat in the tub together as I rubbed her back and she laid against my chest. She came over after running around all day. Emmanuel told me she stopped off at Raven for about twenty minutes and then left. I was stuck going over new contracts for new vendors we might take on as clients. I ordered her favorite Chinese food and sat out on the patio to watch the stars and have dinner. Then I asked for a dance and gave her a bubble bath to relax.

"Being here with you relaxing in the tub. Nobody's ever done this for me. So thank you, baby," she replied.

"My pleasure, princess," I said and we both laughed at my nickname for her.

"You're never going to let me live that down. I wasn't that much of a diva."

"Baby, the word diva in the dictionary has your photo," I joked.

"I'm pregnant!" she blurted out. I went stiff, removing my arms from around her waist.

She leaned up turning around in the tub to face me.

"Wow..."

"I know this is a surprise and I'm not expecting you to be there for me."

"Hold on, wait a minute, Lauren."

Lauren started tearing up and trying to get out of the tub. I grabbed her waist and pulled her back down.

"Stop running from me. Give me a second to take it in, you just sprang it on me."

"Okay."

"Baby, stop crying. I love you and I want this baby."

"You do?"

"Listen, it caught me off guard and will probably take me a little time to get my mind wrapped around the idea of being a father, but yes, I'm happy about this and want to be with you."

"Danielle offered me another contract."

"For how long?'

"It would be for ten years with over twenty exclusive products and a holiday collection."

"What about the baby?" I inquired, all the travel she did in the past wouldn't cut it now.

"She knows and said I can take whatever breaks I need when I get closer to the due date," she replied.

"Then I say sign and follow your dreams, baby. I'm not going anywhere. Who knows, maybe I'll retire and become the next social media star," I teased, kissing her cheek.

One week later, I sat around with Mark and Emmanuel drinking at his place. Charlie was out shopping with Lauren as well as Novah and Danielle. They'd become close over the past few days after we had dinner at Mark's place and he introduced her to his wife. We heard a knock on the door and the last person I expected to see walked inside. I smiled standing up to shake his hand, and he pulled me into a one arm hug.

"Shooter, nice to see you," Jackson said. I faked like I was boxing him, and they chuckled.

"Muffin, when did you get in town?" I asked, sitting back down in my seat.

"We flew in this morning. Catherine's at the hotel with the kids. I decided to come check in on you guys," Jackson said, giving Emmanuel and Mark a handshake.

"Have a seat," Mark told him.

"What's the topic of conversation, you look like a bunch of gossiping girls," Jackson joked.

I waved him off.

"You want something to drink?" Mark asked, jumping up to refill his glass.

"Water is fine," Jackson replied.

"I was filling them in on our plans for the security business."

"Are you finally expanding?" Jackson questioned.

I nodded yes and smirked, taking a sip of my scotch.

"California," I told him.

Jackson's eyebrow rose in shock.

"I did the same then, when he told me," Mark chortled.

"We're doing more international clients and large conglomerates. We do have a case with the King of Monaco wanting to hire us. He's planning a tour of America and the UK," Emmanuel informed him.

"Do you need backup? We're there if you need us, Shooter," Jackson advised.

"I don't think so, I just got the case a few days ago. I'll keep you updated though."

"You know your brothers are always here for you."

"Frogmen for life," Mark announced, raising his glass in the air.

CHAPTER TWENTY-SEVEN

Dominic

She didn't let my past become our reality, and even though I was afraid of our outcome, I allowed my heart to open up to another woman, and she'd become the best thing to happen to me. I watched as she spoke with her friends and family. I had Danielle help me throw a twenty-sixth birthday party with the team from Raven Cosmetics, as well as a few fans that we vetted with a background check through Cole Security Firm. I started the preliminary stage of getting a second company off the ground. After helping Mark and Jackson out for so many years, I discussed with Emmanuel about having a security firm that handled sports stars and major events. Jacinda could have cost me so much if I didn't decide to go after what I wanted and needed. She raised her eyes to find me watching her. I winked at her, and she blushed, blowing a kiss back.

Mark came over as I stood near the bar and ordered a drink. He turned with his back to the bar and arms stretched out, facing the room. I rented the Ocean View Hotel for the party once she finished up her radio interviews.

"I see that look in your eye," Mark commented, voice calm, gaze steady on Charlie as her head tilted back in laughter at something Catherine said.

"See what?" I asked, sipping on the beer bottle.

"Your future. The determination to make everything work and keep her happy no matter what, brings you peace when nothing else is keeping you sane. I've had those moments, and Jackson told me you still have a few sleepless nights because of past missions," Mark told me.

I ran a hand down my face, sighing at the thoughts tearing at my insides. Lauren walked up right as I was about to answer.

"Hey, you. Come dance with me," she stated, entwining our hands, kissing me on the lips.

"Baby, it's your day. You don't want me embarrassing you," I answered. She smoothed her hand down my jacket and I toyed with a lock of her hair.

Lauren grinned, shaking her head and snapping her fingers to the beat of Beyonce.

"This is my song, and I want to dance with my man."

"What am I going to do with you?" I let out a mirthless chuckle.

"The only thing you know how to do. Love me," she stated, rising on her tippy toes capturing my lips. I gripped her by the waist, pulling her in close. She wrapped her arms around my neck.

I heard someone clearing their throat.

"That can wait until after the party, sharpshooter." Mark laughed, patting me on the back and walking off.

The song was fast, but we continued dancing slowly as the crowd took pictures and cheered.

As the night went on, we continued to party and had a good time until we were the only ones left in the room.

...

"Undress for me."

I rented a penthouse suite so we wouldn't need to leave after drinking and dancing all night. She stepped back, biting her bottom lip while removing the red spaghetti strap dress. Starting from her feet, I slowly took in her naked body—every curve that I craved whenever she was near me. Lauren turned and walked off toward the bedroom. I took the last sip of champagne and sat the glass down on the table. I removed my jacket and tie and followed behind her. Entering our bedroom, I shut the door behind me, and she stood in front of me, unbuckling my pants.

Her lips pressed against mine. "I want to thank you for my birthday party." My hands explored the hollows of her back. Lauren dropped to her knees; the touch of her hand was suddenly unbearable in its tenderness as my head fell back in arousal.

"Baby, you know this drives me crazy when your lips are wrapped-"

Her eyes fluttered as she took my dick into her mouth, easing one hand up my stomach.

"Shit, Lauren!"

"Mmmmm..."

"Stop, baby," I pleaded, gripping her shoulders to stand, and she shook her head no.

This was about her tonight, and she mischievously turned it around on me. I caressed her cheek, catching her eyes as my breath quickened.

"Stand up," I demanded, easing my dick out of her mouth.

Lauren got up and crawled on top of the bed with her back to me. Walking up behind her, I needed to be inside her, but I needed to taste her. At the slow penetration of my tongue, she shivered in my arms.

"Ohhh. Dominic!"

I loved her gasps and moans she made.

"Feed me," I demanded. She convulsed around me

as my fingers softly caressed her body. Penetrating her walls, she clenched around me in response. I tossed my head back and moaned as I felt at home.

"Ahhhh...God...Dominic, baby, please," she cried out, gripping the sheets. Stroking her slowly, I wanted tonight to be memorable for us as a couple. Knowing how we started as a couple the first time running into each other at the elevator with me thinking she was a pampered princess and self-involved, and her thinking I was this crazy, overbearing, buttoned-up asshole, and now she was going to be my wife. I wouldn't change a thing.

EPILOGUE

Dominic

Four months later, after all of the craziness, things are better for us. The smile in her eyes contained a sensual flame. The flight didn't take long, and we flew in early from Virginia last night and stayed at our place in Chelsea. She could barely keep her eyes open from the long photoshoot and interviews. Right now, we're up bright and early in Times Square for her to go on air. I put my hand on her shoulder in a possessive gesture. She leaned her head back and gazed into my eyes. I kissed her lips, smothering a groan; she stepped back to put space between us, wiping the lipstick off my lips. Over the past few months, we moved in together, and I let Emmanuel handle more of the day-to-day business with our firm. After speaking with Jackson and Mark, I decided to stick close to Lauren throughout her pregnancy rather than travel with other clients. Opening a second branch in New York did help since her family was based there. Anytime she needed to go do press between Virginia and New York, it wouldn't take long on a private jet. Her parents even bought a house.

"I promise I won't take long. We only have three promo stops, then we can go home," Lauren said, fixing my tie. I smiled, lifting her chin to place a kiss on her lips, caressing her engagement ring.

"My little princess needs to rest," I spoke, rubbing her six months pregnant stomach. We found out we were having a baby girl a month ago, and I told Danielle and the whole team she was not finishing the full tour stops in Europe. Already she flew from California to New York and Chicago doing press over the past two weeks and it was my job to know when to step in to keep her focused on taking care of herself. I was proud of what she'd accomplished with the Lauren Armstrong makeup brand, but this was our time to sit back and enjoy each other without the world having an opinion on our lives.

She wore a light blue long sweater dress with knee high boots. She was about to do a morning interview with CBX Morning News about the launch of her line. The baby gave her a glow; I couldn't help but keep my hands on her at all times. The way her hips spread, and extra weight that had her self-conscious, but I loved when her thick brown thighs were wrapped around me in bed at night.

"I need to get something to eat after this. I'm starving," Lauren said, leaning into my chest with her head down. They had us in the dressing room waiting while they finished one segment with an upcoming actor.

"You want me to send someone to get you something?" I questioned.

She shook her head no. "I ate some of the fruit and a muffin. It shouldn't take long to do this interview."

"Let's hope so. Did I forget to mention I'm proud of you, baby? Your work ethic is amazing, and I can't wait for our little girl to turn out just like her momma."

"You say that now, wait until she runs up your shopping bill," she joked.

"Anything that makes my princess happy," I teased, kissing the tip of her nose.

"You're going to be the best father in the world. Thank you for not giving up on us."

"This was meant to be and you exposed me to what love really means," I spoke right as a knock on the door came and she was told it was time to do the interview. I let her walk ahead of me as I watched her fans scream and shout in the audience as she waved and signed a few autographs. She shook hands with the three hosts, and I stood off to the edge as the light beamed down on her, and her bright smile showed.

THE END

BONUS SCENE

To my Love and protector,

I've been sitting here trying to figure out how to explain to you what the last five years have been like being a wife and mother to our kids. We both know when we first met, it wasn't love at first sight. I'm giggling just thinking about how we bumped into each other at the elevator, and I complain about your elevator etiquette. From then on, it was a Love and hate type of relationship, but somehow the Love overpowered everything else. I admire the man you've become, from being a father to our three kids, the supportive husband taking the backseat to me flying around the world as I follow my dreams. I was watching your dreams come to fruition after being in the navy.

I am so thankful to stand by your side on this

journey called life because I know I'm not the most attentive person when I get into business mode, but you've helped me grow as a woman, wife, and mother. You are a blessing, and I appreciate your corny jokes and witnessing the brief moments of us connecting by sitting and talking together on the couch when the kids go to sleep.

I love you and cherish you with all of my heart.

Love,

Lauren

THE SALVATION SOCIETY

Thank you for reading, we hope you enjoyed this Salvation Society novel. Click on the link below to become a member of the Society and keep up with your beloved SEALs.

Join the Society:

https://www.subscribepage.com/SSsignup

Stay in touch with Chiquita:

https://www.chiquitadennie.com

Check out these books in the Salvation Society available now!

Trap by Jennifer Rebecca

Irreverent by Skye Callahan

Redemption by Laura Lee

Endurance by Alexandra Silva

Exposed by Chiquita Dennie

Want to see what else is coming from The Salvation Society?
Click below for a complete list of titles:
https://www.thesalvationsociety.com/all-books/

BOOKS BY CHIQUITA DENNIE

Catalogue of Releases

Temptation

Antonio & Sabrina: Struck in Love, Books 1, 2, 3, 4

Janice & Carlo: Captivated by His Love

Heart of Stone, Book 1: Emery & Jackson

Heart of Stone, Book 1.5: Emery & Jackson, A Valentine's Day Short Story

Heart of Stone, Book 2: Jordan & Damon

Heart of Stone, Book 3: Angela & Brent

I Deserve His Love-A Second Chance Romance

Bottoms Up-A Heart of Stone Short Book 3.5

Antonio De Luca- The Early Years

Cocky Catcher

Bossy Billionaire

Heart of Stone Book, 4 Jessica and Joseph

Latest Releases:

The Early Years-A Prequel Short story

Antonio and Sabrina: Struck in Love 1, 2, 3, 4

Heart of Stone, Book 1 (Emery and Jackson)

Heart of Stone Book 1.5 Emery & Jackson A Valentine's Day Short

Janice and Carlo: Captivated By His Love

Heart of Stone, Book 2 (Jordan and Damon)

Temptation

Heart of Stone, Book 3 (Angela and Brent)

Cocky Catcher

Bossy Billionaire

Bottoms Up-a Heart of Stone Short 3.5

Love Shorts: A Collection of Short Stories

Joaquin Fuertes-The Fuertes Cartel (Antonio and Sabrina Struck In Love Book 1)

Upcoming Releases (2021):

Joaquin Fuertes-The Fuertes Cartel (Antonio and Sabrina Struck In Love Book 2)

Heart of Stone, Book 4 Jessica and Jordan

She's All I Need

Summer Break Series

Refuel (The Driven World)

Pressure (The Driven World)

EXPOSED PLAYLIST

1. Beyonce-Flaws and All
2. Aaliyah-Are you Feelin Me
3. Aaliyah-Rock The Boat
4. Alicia Keys-Put it In A Love Song
5. Usher-U Got It Bad
6. Jennifer Hudson- Walk It Out
7. Jill Scott-He Love Me

ACKNOWLEDGMENTS

I want to thank my team, who helps me behind the scenes, from my editors to my test readers and graphic designers, and the list goes on. I truly appreciate each of you for keeping me on my toes.

ABOUT THE AUTHOR

A Best-Selling Author and Award-Winning Filmmaker. Her first short film "Invisible" was released in Summer 2017 and screened in multiple festivals and won for Best Short Film. Also, hosts a podcast that showcases the latest in Beauty, Business, and Community called "Moscato and Tea." Her debut release of Antonio and Sabrina Struck In Love has opened a new avenue of writing that she loves.

If you want to know when the next book will come out, please visit Chiquita's website at http://www.chiquitadennie.com, where you can sign up to receive an email for her next release.

Want to know what happens next? Follow me at the links below to catch the next release.

Thank you so much for reading, and if you enjoyed the crazy ride and decided to leave a review, we'd truly appreciate the support. Reviews are the lifeblood of the publishing world. They're read, appreciated, and needed. Please consider taking the time to leave a few words on Goodreads or BookBub.

Sign up for updates and sneak peeks at the sites below:

www.chiquitadennie.com
www.304publishing.com
www.bookbub.com/chiquitadennie
www.goodreads.com/author/chiquitadennie
Facebook.com/chiquitassteamyreadinggroup
www.Twitter.com/304_publishing
www.Instagram.com/304publishing
www.Facebook.com/authorchiquitadennie
www.304publishing.tumblr.com

READER QUESTIONS

1. Should Emmanuel and Novah get a story?
2. Should Lauren and Dominic get a second book?
3. Can Dominic get over the limelight that comes with being with Lauren?
4. What's the name of Lauren's makeup line with Raven Cosmetics?
5. What's the name of Dominic's company?

CPSIA information can be obtained
at www.ICGtesting.com
Printed in the USA
JSHW051451050323
38376JS00005B/136